BREAKAWAY

MICHAEL BETCHERMAN

This book was first published by the Penguin Group (Canada), a division of Pearson Canada Inc. 90 Eglinton Avenue East, Suite 700, Toronto, Ontario, Canada M4P 2Y3

FOR CLAUDETTE AND LAURA

MICHAEL BETCHERMAN is an award-winning screenwriter and author with numerous credits in both documentary and dramatic television. He is the author of two young-adult novels, *Breakaway,* which was shortlisted for the John Spray Mystery Award, and *Face-Off,* which was published by Penguin Group (Canada) in 2014. He is also the author of two online novels, *The Daughters of Freya* and *Suzanne.* Betcherman lives in Toronto with his wife and daughter.

CHAPTER ONE

Nick sat in the front row of the courtroom. His heart pounded as the judge turned toward the jury foreman. "Has the jury reached a verdict?" he asked.

The foreman stood up. "We have, Your Honor. We find the defendant, Steven Macklin, guilty of murder in the first degree."

Nick jumped to his feet. "No!" he screamed.

Nick woke with a start. But waking didn't end the nightmare. It never did. Because he hadn't invented the scene in the courtroom; it had really happened. And Steven Macklin, the man who was convicted of murder, wasn't an imaginary character he'd dreamed up. He was Nick's father.

Nick swung his legs over the side of the bed. The sun streamed through a crack in the blinds. It should have been a welcome sight after the rainiest October in Vancouver history, but Nick didn't notice. His mind was still back in the courtroom, on that day eleven months ago when his life had fallen apart.

He and his father only had enough time for a quick goodbye after the verdict was announced. Nick tried not to cry but he couldn't help it. He buried his head in his dad's chest, hiding his tears, and held on until the guard tapped him on the shoulder and said it was time to go.

"I love you, Nick," his father whispered, his voice cracking with emotion. He gave his son a final squeeze, then stepped back and looked Nick in the eyes. "Be strong, son," he said, his voice once again firm and steady.

"But it's not fair, Dad. It's not fair," Nick cried. "You didn't do it."

"That's what we're going to prove," his dad said confidently, "and as soon as we do, I'll be back home."

But his dad still wasn't home, and they were no closer to finding out who really killed Marty Albertson than they had been the day he went to jail. All Nick knew now was what he knew then; that his dad was an innocent man.

Nick's thoughts were interrupted by a knock on the door. "Time to get up, Nick, or you'll be late for school," Helen called out.

"I'm up," he shouted irritably. He heard Helen's footsteps disappear down the hallway. He knew he shouldn't have yelled at her. He should be grateful that she and Al had taken him in. But it was hard to feel grateful about anything while his father was behind bars. Check that. It wasn't hard; it was impossible.

His dad first raised the subject of Nick's living arrangements during the trial. They were in the kitchen playing backgammon, as they had hundreds of times before. "We need to have a back-up plan in case we lose," his father said. "We're not going to lose," Nick replied. He rolled the dice and made his move. "Your turn."

The next time the subject came up, Nick didn't have the luxury of avoiding the conversation. They were in the visiting room at the prison, the day after the verdict came down. "Why can't I stay at home?" Nick asked.

"You're only sixteen," his dad said. "You're too young to live alone. Monique and Dennis want you to go live with them. I think it's a good idea."

Nick disagreed. Uncle Dennis was his mother's brother. Nick liked him and Aunt Monique well enough, although he hadn't seen much of them since they moved to Ontario six years earlier, not long after his mother died. But there was no way—"no effing way" was how he put it at the time—he was going to leave Vancouver and live three thousand miles away from his father.

That left boarding school as the only alternative, and Nick was resigned to going there when Al and Helen Hawkins invited him to come live with them. Al was his father's agent. He'd signed Nick's dad up when he was playing junior hockey, negotiated his first contract with the Vancouver Canucks, and had represented him ever since.

Living with the Hawkins was a more attractive proposition than sharing a dormitory with a roomful of preppy kids, and Nick agreed to move in with them despite one major concern. He'd known Al all his life but if Al thought that gave him the right to act like he was Nick's father just because Nick was living in his house, the two of them were going to have some major problems.

It turned out to be a non-issue. All Al did was lay down a few ground rules. If Nick was going to be out later than midnight, he had to call to let them know where he was. He was expected to help out around the house when he was asked, and he had to be home for Sunday night dinner.

"Personally, I don't give a hoot," Al had said, staring at Nick solemnly, with no trace of the smile that usually appeared on his round face, "but it's important to Helen, so it's important to me."

Nick didn't have a problem with any of that. It wouldn't stop him from doing the only thing that mattered: finding out who really killed Marty Albertson, so his dad could come back home.

CHAPTER TWO

The sun had disappeared by the time Nick got off the bus. As he walked up the stairs to the school's main entrance, it started to rain. McAndrew was standing in the foyer.

"Mr. Macklin. To what do we owe the pleasure?" he asked sarcastically. Nick walked past him without a word.

McAndrew was the vice-principal, which was an unfortunate coincidence for Nick because he also happened to be the coach of the West Vancouver Lightning, the local rep hockey team that Nick had played for. Nick had been one of the team's best players, but he'd quit just before the playoffs the previous March when his father lost his appeal—his last chance to persuade the court he was innocent.

Without Nick in the lineup the Lightning had lost in the finals, and McAndrew had been on his case ever since. If Nick was one minute late for school—and he was usually a lot later than that—McAndrew was sure to give him a detention. That meant he was spending a lot of time in the study hall after school—not that he did much studying there. Doing well in school stopped being a priority the moment his father went to prison. He had barely scraped through grade eleven last year, and this year things looked even worse.

"Tough love" was the way McAndrew described it, but Nick knew that love had nothing to do with it. If he had still been playing hockey, he could have shown up at noon every day and McAndrew wouldn't have said boo.

"I know it can't be easy for you to deal with the situation," McAndrew said when he summoned Nick to his office just after school started, "but it's my job to make sure you get an education and that's what I intend to do."

The *situation*. That was the word everybody used to refer to what had happened. His English teacher, Mr. Putnam, would call it a euphemism—a vague word used to describe something unpleasant to make it seem less real. Like the way people said his mother had "passed away" instead of just coming right out and saying she was dead and gone forever.

It was the same with his dad. Calling what happened to him a *situation* didn't change the fact that he was serving a life sentence in prison for a murder he didn't commit. And nobody, including McAndrew, had a goddamn clue what that felt like.

Nick glanced back at the foyer as he walked into math class. McAndrew was still standing there, staring at him.

At four o'clock Nick left the school after sleepwalking his way through another day of classes. The sun had broken through the clouds. Red, Biggie, and Ivan were down the street, waiting for the bus. Nick couldn't help feeling a little envious as he watched his former teammates joking with each other in their leather jackets with West Vancouver Lightning written on the back. He missed being part of the team, he couldn't deny it. It was like a second family.

That's what his dad always said about playing with the Canucks, and it was why he stayed with them for his whole career, even though he could have made more money with another team. It drove Al Hawkins crazy. "At least pretend you're thinking about playing somewhere else," Al said the last time his father was up for a new contract. "You gotta give me something to work with. If they know you want to stay in Vancouver, they're not going to cough up the do-re-mi." Do-re-mi was Al's corny way of saying money.

His dad just sat there and smiled. "I'm making plenty of money as it is. I don't need more. Nick and I are happy here. Besides, the team has always treated me fairly." Nick didn't think his father would say that now. Even though there were two years left on his five-year guaranteed contract, the conviction gave the team the legal right to terminate their agreement. And they didn't hesitate to use it. That was his dad's reward for sixteen years of uninterrupted service. Al fought them as hard as he could, but legally they were within their rights, and there wasn't much sympathy for a convicted murderer in the court of public opinion.

Google came running up just as the bus arrived. Google, a.k.a. Mark Mandell, had played Atom, Peewee, and Bantam with the guys. When he didn't make the Midget team last year, he signed on as team manager. They called him Google because there wasn't anything about computers that he didn't know.

Nick watched his friends board the bus. The five of them used to be inseparable. If they weren't playing hockey, they were talking about it or watching it on TV. For a moment he imagined he was with them, talking strategy and psyching themselves up for the game, like they'd done so many times in the past.

But that was Before.

Before and After. His life was divided in two, just like world history was divided into BC and AD. But instead of Nick's reference point being the birth of Jesus Christ, it was the day his father had gone to jail.

Nick couldn't remember the last time he'd hung with the guys. It was his own doing. For months they kept calling, but he kept making excuses, and after a while, the phone stopped ringing.

Nick watched the bus pull away. The Lightning had a game that evening against the Burnaby Owls, and his friends were headed to La Fortuna for the pre-game meal. The restaurant was owned by Red's parents and the guys ate there before every home game. It was a tradition. Nick didn't know how many times he'd been at the restaurant, but there was one time he'd never be able to forget. It had started out as one of the happiest days of his life and ended up being one of the worst.

It happened less than two years ago, even though it felt like a century. The Lightning had won the Bantam AA championship. Red's parents hosted a banquet at La Fortuna.

After dinner, they all watched the Canucks' game on TV. It was the last game of the season. Vancouver had already qualified for the playoffs, but the Leafs needed a win or they were out. With a couple of minutes left, the Canucks were leading 3–0. There he was, surrounded by his best buddies, watching his father on TV. The Canucks were going to the playoffs, and the Leafs were going golfing. Life didn't get much sweeter than that.

Then it happened. "The hit."

Nick must have seen it a couple of hundred times in the days after it happened and then a couple of hundred more during the trial. His dad was skating across center ice when the Leafs' Marty Albertson raced up from behind and viciously cross-checked him on the head. His dad went down like he'd been shot. The image of him lying there, crumpled on the ice was seared into Nick's memory. His father was in a coma for a week. The doctors weren't sure if he would ever walk again. To their amazement he was back on his feet in two months, but there was no question of him ever playing hockey again.

Albertson was suspended for thirty games. Thirty measly games for one of the dirtiest hits in hockey history! The day the league made the announcement, a reporter for a local TV station asked Nick's dad for his reaction. Enraged, he said Albertson should have been thrown in jail and barred from hockey for life. Nick had never seen his father so angry.

Five months later Marty Albertson was dead, and Nick's dad was charged with his murder. At the trial his furious reaction to Albertson's suspension came back to haunt him. The Crown Attorney said it explained why he killed him. "You don't have to look very hard to find a motive in this case," he told the jury. "When the league didn't stop Marty Albertson from playing hockey, Steve Macklin decided to do it himself."

The case against his dad was simple enough. Albertson had played with the Canucks before he was traded to the Leafs, and he still lived in Vancouver during the off-season. On the morning of September 18, his body was found in his condo by a man he'd hired to paint the living room. Albertson was slumped in an armchair with one bullet in his head and another in his heart.

The autopsy report said he died sometime between four and seven the previous evening. When the police found an entry in Albertson's BlackBerry showing he had scheduled a meeting with Steve Macklin at five p.m. that day, they gave Nick's father a call.

Nick's dad told the police that Albertson called him around four p.m. and asked if they could meet to talk about what happened. The call came out of the blue. It was the first time they had spoken since "the hit." That was a real sore point with Nick's dad, especially since the two of them had been teammates before Albertson was traded to the Leafs. The Crown Attorney used that against him at the trial as well.

Nick's father said Albertson was supposed to come to their house in West Van at five p.m. but he never showed. He said he waited around until six-thirty, and then he left the house for a fundraising event at a hospital in downtown Vancouver.

The police didn't believe him. According to Albertson's BlackBerry, the meeting was to take place at his condo, not at the Macklin house in West Van. The police examined the clothes Nick's dad was wearing the night of the murder and found a small trace of beige paint on the back of his suit jacket, up near his shoulder. When tests proved the paint on his jacket matched the fresh paint in Albertson's living room, he was arrested.

At first Nick's dad couldn't explain how the paint ended up on his jacket. He claimed he'd never even been to Albertson's condo. Then he remembered that he had spoken to a man—a bald man—as he went into the washroom just before the fundraiser started. The man had approached him from behind, tapped him on his shoulder to get his attention, told him he was a big fan—and then limped away. Nick's dad said the bald man must have put the paint on his jacket when he tapped him on his shoulder.

The police didn't buy the explanation, and when the detectives Nick's dad hired couldn't find the bald man with a limp, neither did the jury.

CHAPTER THREE

It took Nick nearly forty-five minutes to get from school to the corner of Granville Street and West Broadway, where he boarded the 99 bus heading west. He hadn't been on that one for a while. He sat down at a window seat on the curb side so that he could get a good look at the pedestrians as they strolled along. He was looking for the bald man with the limp—Baldy, Nick called him. He was the key to the case, the key to proving his dad didn't kill Marty Albertson. Nick had been looking for him ever since his father went to jail.

He took the bus all the way to Alma, then got off and took the one going back the way he'd come. As they passed Cypress Street, Nick saw a man in a leather jacket limping along the sidewalk in front of Kinko's. When he took his baseball cap off and scratched his bald head, Nick jumped to his feet, pushed the stop button, and hurried to the rear door.

He tried to keep his eyes on the man, but by the time he hopped off the bus at Burrard he'd lost sight of him. Nick ran back along West Broadview and stopped in front of Kinko's, but the bald man was nowhere to be seen. He was about to give up when the man came out of a convenience store up the street. He unwrapped a pack of cigarettes, lit a smoke, and headed in Nick's direction. Nick turned his back to him, took out his cellphone, put it on camera mode, and held it up to his ear as if he was talking to someone. When the bald man entered the frame, Nick snapped his picture.

He followed the guy along West Broadway until he turned right on Arbutus, walked down to West 7th and entered a low-rise apartment building. Nick took a notebook out of his knapsack and wrote down the address. Then he walked back to the bus stop on Broadway.

The man Nick had just photographed was Baldy Number Six. Nick had shown photos of the other five to his dad but none of them were the right guy. It was hard not to be discouraged but as his dad always said, winners never quit and quitters never win. As long as his father was in jail, Nick wasn't going to stop looking.

He felt like Harrison Ford in *The Fugitive*. Ford plays a doctor who escapes from prison after being wrongly convicted of murdering his wife, and spends the rest of the movie looking for the one-armed man who killed her. The only difference was that Nick wasn't playing a part in a movie.

He saw *The Fugitive* with his dad on "movie night." Movie night was a family tradition they'd started when his mom got sick. Once a week they took turns choosing a movie, then they'd order takeout and watch the film together. Nick and his dad continued the tradition after his mom died.

The Fugitive was his father's choice for movie night. The day after they watched it, Marty Albertson was murdered, and the day after that, his dad was charged with the crime.

Nick sat at the rear of the bus as it headed east on Broadway, his eyes moving between the photo of Baldy Number Six on his cellphone and a laminated drawing of a bald man that he kept in his knapsack.

The drawing was an artist's sketch of Baldy, based on his father's description of the man he had seen at the hospital. There hadn't been much for the artist to go on. All his dad could remember was that the man was thin, between thirty and fifty years old, and had a round face. The fact that Baldy Number Six fit this vague description didn't mean much, but Nick felt a surge of excitement as he zoomed in on the man's face and saw the cross earring dangling from his left ear.

His dad had always said there was something missing in the artist's sketch, some detail about the man's face that he just couldn't recall. Nick stared at the earring. It was exactly the kind of thing you'd notice when you saw it, he thought, but you might not remember later. As soon as he got back to the house he'd print up the photo and mail it to his father so it would arrive in time for Nick's visit to the prison on Saturday.

Nick snapped his cellphone shut. He had a good feeling about Baldy Number Six. A real good feeling.

CHAPTER FOUR

On Friday afternoon Nick was sitting in English class, watching the hands on the clock inch their way toward three-thirty and counting the hours until he would get to see his dad.

"Not one of your best efforts," Mr. Putnam said as he handed Nick his essay on *Hamlet*. D minus was written in red on the cover page. "It would have helped if you'd actually read the play, instead of relying on Spark Notes."

Nick knew Putnam wasn't being a hard-ass. He was just frustrated that Nick's grades had dropped from straight As to straight Ds, and like most of his other teachers, he was hoping that Nick would bring them up to where they were before.

"To study or not to study, that is the question," Nick said.

Putnam laughed along with the rest of the class, then whispered so that only Nick could hear him. "Class clown doesn't suit you, Nick."

Nick shoved his essay into his knapsack as Putnam moved on to the next student. He glanced over at Ivan who was sitting beside him, staring out the window, lost in thought. Nick knew he was thinking about today's game against Hollyburn, the Lightning's perennial rival and the team that defeated them in the finals last year. He knew exactly how Ivan was feeling. He remembered what it was like to sit in class on the day of a big game. You were so nervous and excited that it was impossible to concentrate on schoolwork. Every minute seemed to last an hour. All you could think about was getting on the ice so that the butterflies in your stomach would finally go away.

The bell rang, bringing Nick back to the present. Chairs scraped on the linoleum floor as the students got to their feet. A dozen conversations started up. Putnam's voice broke through the clamor. "Pick up one of these on your way out." He waved a stack of papers in the air. "'Do Not Go Gentle into that Good Night' by Dylan Thomas. I want an analysis of the poem for Monday. Maximum two pages, double-spaced." A collective groan greeted the announcement.

"What's the minimum?" asked Fred Feldman. When it came to being the class clown, Fred had the role all locked up. The only thing he was serious about was snowboarding.

"Whatever you hand in, I suspect." said Putnam.

"Less is more," said Fred, quoting one of Putnam's favorite expressions, meaning that one clearly written sentence was better than a lot of vague ones that didn't say much. The class laughed. Fred leaned across the aisle and high-fived his best friend, Donnie Keagan.

"Unfortunately, Mr. Feldman, in your case less is usually less," Putnam replied without missing a beat. Everybody laughed again, including Fred. He didn't mind being the butt of Putnam's joke as long as it put him in the spotlight. As Donnie Keagan put it, Fred would stab his mother just to get the attention.

Ivan slung his knapsack over his shoulder. "See you later," he said to Nick.

"Yeah. Good luck tonight."

Ivan nodded. He didn't have to say he wished Nick

were playing. Nick knew he was thinking it. The last time they talked about it was a month ago, just before the hockey season started. Ivan asked Nick if he was ready to join the team again. When Nick said he just didn't have the heart—not while his dad was still in jail—Ivan understood, but he couldn't hide his disappointment. The two of them had been teammates since they were nine years old. They both knew this was probably the last chance they would ever have to play together again.

Nick collected his books and stuffed them into his knapsack. He walked to the front of the classroom, took a Dylan Thomas handout from Putnam's desk, and headed for the door. Sherry was sitting at her desk in the front row. She didn't look up as he passed by.

Sherry was also part of Before. Nick had met her on the first day of high school. Well, kind of met her. She was sitting beside him in the auditorium as the principal welcomed the new students. The first thing Nick noticed was her hair. It was the reddest hair he had ever seen, and it hung halfway down her back. The second thing he noticed was her T-shirt. It had the words YOU PEOPLE ARE KILLING ME above a picture of the globe. He thought that was pretty cool. When she looked toward him and gave him a smile, he felt as though his heart was going to explode. He wanted to say something but he couldn't even manage "Hello." He sat there for the entire assembly feeling like a total loser. When it ended, he summoned up his nerve and turned to speak to her. But she was talking to a friend and the moment was lost. Ten minutes later he went into his homeroom and there she was again. Her name was called out right before his when the teacher took attendance. Sherry Lawrence.

15

Whenever she looked his way he practically swallowed his tongue. It was a week or so before he actually spoke to her. It wasn't what you'd call a Kodak moment. He was horsing around in the hallway with Biggie and Google when he lost his balance and bumped into her, sending her books flying all over the floor. He picked them up and handed them to her. "Sorry," he said, feeling foolish, and then, desperately trying to be cool, proceeded to make a complete ass of himself. "Don't I know you from somewhere?"

Sherry gave him a scornful look and turned to her friend Vanessa. "Did you hear that? It talks." Then she walked away, her red hair bouncing.

"Don't I know you from somewhere?" Biggie mocked. "I gotta remember that one." Google laughed. Nick punched him in the shoulder.

"What did you do that for?" Google asked, rubbing his shoulder. "I didn't say anything."

Nick looked up at Biggie. Way up. He wasn't called Biggie for nothing. Then he looked down at Google. "'Cause I'm not stupid," he answered.

"That's a matter of opinion," said Google.

Nick called Sherry that same night. There were five Lawrence's listed in the telephone directory for West Vancouver, but he didn't have to look any further than the first name on the list. A. Lawrence. The *A*, Nick later learned, stood for Alison, Sherry's mom.

"Hello."

"May I speak to Sherry please?"

"This is Sherry."

"Hi, Sherry, this is 'It'." She laughed, and he fell in love with her right then and there. They were together for a little over two years, until his father was convicted. Nick never officially broke up with her, he just stopped calling her. She finally confronted him one day outside of school. "Don't shut me out, Nick. I'm here for you. I want to help," she said. But he was way past wanting anything from anybody—or being able to accept anything either. He just stood there, stone-faced, until she walked away. He knew she deserved better than that but he just couldn't help himself.

Dr. Davis, a shrink Nick saw for a few months after his dad went to prison, said he did it because he was afraid she'd leave him, just like everyone else had. It took Nick a while to wrap his head around that one. His mom didn't leave him: she died. And his dad didn't leave him either. He was taken away. But even if Davis was right, it didn't make any difference to the way he felt. Lately he'd been thinking about giving Sherry a call—he'd been thinking about it a lot—but he hadn't been able to actually pick up the phone and punch in her number. Anyway, it was probably too late. Ivan said his girlfriend, Jennifer, had seen Sherry a couple of times at the mall at Park Royal, holding hands with a guy in a University of British Columbia jacket.

CHAPTER FIVE

It was still dark outside when Nick woke up on Saturday morning. He looked at the clock on his bedside table. It was ten to seven. He'd lain awake most of the night, listening to the rain beating on the roof, trying not to think about Baldy Number Six and his cross earring, but unable to think about anything else.

Al was standing by the breakfast table when Nick came into the kitchen, yakking away even though nobody else was in the room. Nick thought he was talking to himself until he realized Al was on the phone. That wasn't surprising, even though it was early Saturday morning. Nick was pretty sure Al slept with his Bluetooth earpiece on.

"I hear you, dude," Al said. He called all his clients dude. Nick wondered if he knew how ridiculous he sounded. When the few hairs you've got left are grey, you shouldn't be using the word *dude*. Even if you do have the phone numbers of most of the league's best players on speed dial.

"Of course you're worth more than Morrison," Al said. "He can't carry your jock. But there's nothing we can do until your contract is up. I can understand why you're upset, but this is good news," Al said. "All they've done is raise the bar for when your turn comes around. Hit the weights, dude. You're going to need to bulk up to carry all that do-re-mi they're going to give you ... All right. Speak

18

to you later."

Al turned to Nick and put on a thick Russian accent. "I skate faster, I shoot harder. Why Morrison make more money than me?" If Nick didn't have his eyes open, he would have sworn Vladimir Medkov, the Canucks' all-star defenseman, was in the room. Al had him pegged perfectly. He was amazing that way. All he had to do was hear someone talk once and he could imitate him perfectly.

One time, when Nick's dad was going through the worst slump of his career, Al called him and pretended he was the Canuck's coach, Ed Morgan. He told him he was being sent down to their farm team, the Manitoba Moose. Nick's father fell for it hook, line, and sinker. He was so furious he said he was quitting the team. Al let him rant and rave for a while before he put an end to the prank. He must have known what he was doing because that night Nick's dad scored two goals against the Islanders, including the game winner.

Al's phone rang again. "Hey. What's up? ... Hang on. I gotta go outside. You're breaking up," Al said. He turned to Nick as he opened the French doors leading to the patio. "You know I'm taking you to see your dad?" he said.

Nick nodded. Al never complained, but Nick knew he wasn't thrilled about it. Not that he blamed him. It was a two-hour drive to the prison, two more for the visit, and another two to get back home. That meant Al's day was shot. Nick wasn't allowed to go the prison by himself because he was a minor. He could only go when Al or Helen—usually Helen—could take him. It was one of a million prison rules designed to make life harder than it already was. Al and Helen made sure Nick saw his father once a month. That wasn't nearly enough, but he couldn't expect them to do any more.

Al glanced at his watch. "We'll leave in fifteen minutes," he said, hitching his pants up over his round belly.

"Sounds good ... dude," Nick said. Al ignored the sarcasm and stepped out onto the patio, closing the French doors behind him. Nick opened the fridge and took out a container of yogurt. It was organic, of course. Everything Helen bought was organic—fruit, vegetables, even Alfie's cat food. It drove Al crazy. "You could feed an army for the amount it costs to feed that damn cat," he'd say whenever he looked at the grocery bill.

It was kind of funny. Al didn't mind spending a hundred thousand bucks on his Lexus Sports Coupe but he'd rant and rave about paying a few extra dollars for organic cat food. Nick looked out at the patio through the floor-to-ceiling windows in the kitchen. Al was pacing beside the swimming pool, arms waving, talking a mile a minute. The pool extended out over a cliff above the Pacific Ocean. When the sun was out, Bowen Island was visible in the distance. It was the kind of view you'd see in a James Bond movie. *Al can afford organic cat food,* Nick thought. *Hell, he can afford to fill the pool with it.*

Helen came into the kitchen, her trim figure clad in a yoga outfit. "Morning," she said. Her short blond hair was still wet from her morning shower.

"Morning."

Helen looked at Nick's bowl of yogurt. "Is that all you're eating? There's some of the granola you like in the cupboard. And fresh fruit salad in the fridge."

"Is it organic?"

"Very funny," she said with a smile as she walked to the counter. A half-dozen vitamin containers sat on a tray. She took a pill out of each container, poured herself a glass of water, and swallowed the vitamins one after another. She checked the time.

"Oh my God. Is that the time?" she said. "I have to be in Kitsilano by eight."

"That's a long way to go for a yoga class."

"It's a master class. The instructor's come all the way from India."

Sherry was into yoga too. She'd dragged Nick to a class once. He thought it was going to be a breeze. Compared to doing wind sprints in full hockey gear, a little stretching didn't sound like much of a workout. "I can already touch my toes," he said to Sherry dismissively when the class started. He was singing a different tune by the time it ended. That night they went to the movies, and afterwards he was so stiff he could barely get out of his seat. Sherry got a big kick out of that. "Okay, Macklin," she said, "let's see you touch your toes now."

Sherry always called him by his last name. He thought that was pretty cool. It was like she was saying they weren't just boyfriend and girlfriend, they were buddies too. The only other girl who'd ever called him by his last name was Sherry's friend Vanessa. It wasn't so cool that time. It happened a month or so after he had frozen Sherry out of his life. He was sitting by himself in the Starbucks in Park Royal, when Sherry and Vanessa walked in. As soon as Sherry saw him, she left the café. Vanessa marched over to his table and got right into his face. "You're an asshole, Macklin," she said. She stared at him, daring him to deny it. He didn't say a word. What could he say? She was right. He was an asshole.

Helen went over to the window and knocked on it to get Al's attention. He answered her goodbye wave with a big smile and a wave of his own. She turned toward Nick.

"Gotta run. Give my love to your dad. I left the books he wanted by the front door. You'll need a box for them, but you can buy one at the post office."

"Okay," Nick said. He would have to mail the books to his father, just like he had to mail the photo of Baldy. Visitors weren't allowed to bring anything into the prison. The authorities claimed it was for security reasons, but as far as Nick was concerned it was just another one of their pointless rules.

He took out his cellphone and scrolled down to the photo of Baldy Number Six. He zoomed in on the cross earring. Maybe he and his dad wouldn't have to put up with those rules for too much longer.

CHAPTER SIX

Nick sat on the front steps waiting for Al. He looked through the books Helen had bought for his father. They were all about meditation. *Journey to the Heart. How to Achieve Inner Peace. Wherever You Go, There You Are.*

His dad had started meditating about a month ago. "It helps me control my anger," he explained when Nick asked him about it, "and that makes it a lot easier to deal with the situation." The *situation*. There was that word again. Nick nodded, but as far as he was concerned his dad could meditate until he was blue in the face but it wouldn't change a damn thing. There was only one way of dealing with the *situation*. Putting an end to it.

His cellphone rang. He checked the caller ID. It was Google, calling to give him the results of the Lightning's game against Hollyburn.

"Hey," Nick said. "How did we do?" *Funny how I say we,* he thought. Even though he wasn't playing anymore, Nick still felt like he was part of the team.

"We got killed. 7-2. We were never in the game. If we keep playing like this, we won't even make the playoffs."

The loss dropped the team's record to one and four, their only victory coming in the game against Burnaby earlier that week. The fact that the team was doing so poorly made Nick feel guilty. But the thought of playing again while his dad was in jail ... he couldn't. He just couldn't. *Then again, maybe Dad won't be in jail too much longer,* he thought. He debated telling Google about Baldy Number Six but decided not to. If this was the guy they were looking for, Google would find out soon enough.

Google was the only one of his friends who knew Nick was still looking for Baldy. For the first few months after his dad's arrest, they all had helped with the search. They even made up a schedule. None of them cared about the so-called evidence that convinced just about everybody else that his dad was guilty. They knew he was innocent. But eventually Nick told them there was no point in carrying on. "It's like looking for a needle in a haystack," he said. They all said they would be happy to keep looking, but he could tell they were relieved. Nick didn't blame them. It *was* like looking for a needle in a haystack.

He didn't tell his friends that he was going to keep searching because if he did, he knew they would stay on the case too. Google had found out because he bumped into Nick one day on the Fraser Street bus, He knew the only reason for Nick to be in East Van was to look for Baldy. Google agreed not to tell the others as long as Nick understood that he wasn't going to stop searching either.

Google was doing it out of friendship, but Nick knew he enjoyed the hunt. Google was planning to study criminology in university so he could become a spy with CSIS, Canada's intelligence agency. The way Google saw it, looking for Baldy was job training. Nick was glad his friend was still involved. Google knew the case as well as he did, and it made him feel less alone to have someone to talk to.

Nick got to his feet as Al came out the front door. "Gotta go," he said. "Going to see my dad. Later."

"Later."

Al tossed the car keys to him. "You drive," he said.

Nick opened the rear door, grabbed the sign with *L* for Learner on it, and placed it against the rear window.

"When's your road test?" Al asked, as he opened the passenger door.

"About a month from now." A month and ten days, to be precise. December 14, the day he turned seventeen. If he passed the road test, he'd get his permanent license. It would mean he'd be able to drive by himself, instead of having to depend on Al or Helen. Except when he had to go to the prison, of course. It would be another year before he'd be allowed to go there on his own.

He got into the Lexus, moved the seat back and adjusted the mirrors. Then he started the car and drove down the winding driveway to the street. The sky was dark overhead.

"There's a mountain range out there somewhere, but I can't remember the last time I saw it," Al said. "If we want to stop all those Easterners from moving out here, all we have to do is tell them to come visit in November." Al's cellphone rang. "Dude! How's my favorite client?"

Al was still on the phone ten minutes later when Nick passed the sign for the 15th Street exit that led to his old house. Every time he passed it, Nick thought of the countless times he and his dad had taken it to go home. Each time he wondered if they would ever do it again. Well, he didn't have to wonder anymore. The last time he was at the prison, his dad told him he was putting the house up for sale.

Nick could still remember the sick feeling he had in the pit of his stomach when his father broke the news. It was near the end of the visit. "It doesn't make sense to leave it empty," his dad said with a shrug. Nick tried not to let on how upset he was. He'd lived there his whole life, and in his mind, he'd always pictured the two of them back there again when the nightmare finally ended. Selling the house meant that wasn't going to happen, but that wasn't what troubled him. It didn't matter where he and his dad lived as long as they were together. But the decision to sell the house, together with his father's newfound interest in meditation, gave Nick the distinct impression that his dad didn't think they would be back together any time soon.

Al was still yakking away when they reached Burnaby. "Just make sure he doesn't sign with anybody before I get a chance to talk to him. Okay, bye." Al hung up and looked over at Nick. "Slow down, you're driving too fast." Nick checked the speedometer. He was going 70 mph. He eased his foot off the accelerator.

An hour later they passed the turnoff to Chilliwack. "Chilliwack," Al said. "That's where I first saw your dad play." Nick knew the story. Al had told it to him dozen times over the years, but he never tired of hearing it. A good thing too, because once Al started telling a story, there was no stopping him.

"I was working as a scout for the Rangers. I covered all of Western Canada. Spent most of my time in a car. I was in Chilliwack to take a look at a guy named Claude LaRochelle. He was a nice player, plenty of speed, but I thought he was too weak to play in the NHL. It was Steve's first year with Winnipeg. He was raw, but I could see he had the complete package—speed, size, smarts. And guts. Boy, did he have guts. He wouldn't back away from anybody. I spoke to him after the game. We hit it off from the start. When he told me he didn't have an agent, I offered to represent him. We sealed the deal then and there, with a handshake. Never did get around to signing a contract. That night I called Helen and told her that I was going to quit my job with the Rangers and become an agent. She went bananas. Two of the boys were in high school and Jesse had just started university. Helen was sure we were going to end up in the poorhouse. That first year was rough. But by the end of the season, it was clear your dad was going to be drafted in the first round, and once other players knew he'd signed with me, things took off."

Whenever Al told the story, Nick's father always said that wasn't the way it happened. He said he didn't even like Al when he first met him, but after Al called him every day for a month he realized he would never find anybody who would fight harder for him than Al would. "The biggest bullshitter in the world," he used to say about Al, "but he's always had my back."

A visit to the prison didn't go by without his father mentioning how grateful he was to Al for taking Nick into his home. Nick didn't have the heart to tell him that Al actually hadn't been all that keen on the idea. A month or so after he moved in with the Hawkins, he had overheard him and Helen talking by the pool.

"I feel badly for Nick, but he isn't our responsibility," Al said. "We've already raised three children of our own. I was looking forward to the two of us having some time for ourselves."

"I've known Nick since he was a baby," Helen said. "I'm not going to let him live with strangers."

You don't become the most successful agent in professional hockey without recognizing when you've run out of negotiating room. "That's fine with me," Al said. "I just wanted to make sure you were okay with it."

Still, Nick had to admit, Al had stood by his dad when most everybody else had dropped by the wayside. Even though Marty Albertson had been his client too, Al came to the trial every day and never missed an opportunity to tell the press that Nick's dad was an innocent man.

The loyalty cut both ways. About five years earlier, on Al's recommendation, Nick's father and a few of Al's other clients had invested in a resort development in the Philippines. Nick didn't know all the details, but everybody lost a shitload of money. Some of the players were so mad that they left Al for another agent, but his dad stayed with him and persuaded most of the others—including Marty Albertson—to do the same. "Your father saved my ass," Al told Nick on more than one occasion.

Nick didn't know how much his dad had lost. All he said was that it was an expensive lesson. His father was big on lessons. "Everybody makes mistakes," he'd tell Nick. "The difference between a smart person and a stupid one is that a smart person doesn't make the same mistake twice." He said it was his fault for not taking responsibility for his own affairs. He'd invested because Al was putting his own do-re-mi into it, instead of looking into it for himself.

"I'm an incredibly lucky man," he said when Nick asked him why he wasn't more upset about it. "I don't have a right to be upset, not when millions of people in the world don't have a roof over their heads or enough food to eat." His dad didn't just talk the talk, he walked the walk. After "the hit" ended his career, he set up a foundation to help underprivileged kids. He put up a lot of his own money and hoped that his name would persuade other people to donate as well. Of course, that all ended when he went to jail. Nobody was interested in a charity headed by a convicted murderer.

Twenty minutes later they passed the road sign for Agassiz. A few minutes after that they turned onto the side road that led to the prison. It was called Cemetery Road. Whoever called it that has a sick sense of humor, Nick thought.

He pulled into the parking lot of Kent Institution, the maximum-security prison where his dad was being held. Nick and Al got out of the car and walked toward the two-story red brick visitors' center. A chain-link fence topped with barbed wire encircled the entire compound. The squat ugly building where the inmates were housed was a few hundred yards away, across a treeless field. No matter how many times Nick came here, it never seemed any less depressing. There might as well have been a sign: *You are now leaving the world as you know it.*

CHAPTER SEVEN

Nick and Al joined the lineup at the security desk. Even though visiting hours didn't start for another half-hour, there were already about twenty people ahead of them. Visits only lasted an hour and three-quarters, and nobody wanted to miss a minute. There was only one reason why the authorities limited visits to an hour and three-quarters instead of a round number like two hours, Nick thought bitterly. To remind you that they controlled every detail of what goes on in here.

"I'm Nick Macklin," he said when he got to the head of the line. "I'm here to see Steven Macklin."

The guard at the desk consulted his clipboard. "I see a Nicholas Macklin," he said, as if Nicholas and Nick might be two different people.

"That's me," Nick said. "Dickhead," he added under his breath. Most of the guards were actually pretty decent—as long as you followed their orders to the letter. He handed his learner's permit and his student card to the guard without being asked. He knew the drill. Two pieces of photo ID or you wouldn't be allowed in.

The guard studied Nick's photo, then scrutinized Nick, then peered at the photo again, just in case Nick was an imposter who had come to bust his dad out of prison. Nick swallowed his anger. The guard returned his ID along with a visitor's pass and a key to one of the lockers on the other side of the room. "Put the pass on and keep it visible at all times," he said.

Nick clipped the pass to his shirt and walked to his locker. The only items visitors were allowed to bring into the visitors' room were the key and some coins for the vending machines. You could bring in eight dollars worth of coins. Not ten. Eight. Just in case you'd forgotten who was in charge. He took his cellphone out of his jacket pocket. The picture of Baldy with his cross earring was still on the display. He turned the phone off and put it in the locker along with his wallet and the car keys.

Al deposited his belongings in another locker. "I gotta go to the can," he said.

"Okay," Nick said and headed to the drug scanner.

Drugs were a major problem in the prison. No matter what the authorities did, people somehow managed to smuggle them in. The drug scanner was designed to prevent that. It was an upright tube, large enough for a person to walk into, with a computer that could detect tiny amounts of drug residue.

"What a waste of money," a husky man standing in front of Nick muttered in a low voice. "You'd have to be a moron to bring drugs in here with you. There's a million other ways to do it."

"Just be glad you don't have to bend over and spread 'em," said the man standing next to him. Nick knew what he was talking about. After every visit the prisoners were strip-searched to make sure they hadn't been given any contraband. His dad never talked about it, but each time the door to the cells closed behind him, Nick couldn't help imagining what was about to happen on the other side.

After Nick went through the scanner, he joined the lineup at an airport-style metal detector. When it was his turn, he put his coins and the locker key on a tray and walked through the opening. The guard, Leon, looked right through Nick as if he had never seen him before.

Leon was a first-class asshole. His dad warned Nick about him the first time he came to the prison. "There are only two things you say to that prick," his dad cautioned. "'Yes sir' and 'No sir.' Got it?"

"Yes sir," Nick had answered.

Leon passed a wand over Nick's body, then nodded to indicate he could move on. Nick collected his coins and the key and joined the group waiting by the door to the visiting area.

"Hey, Nick. How was the drive?" asked Pete, another prison guard.

"No problem," Nick said. Pete was the only guard Nick truly liked. On Nick's first visit to the prison, Pete made it clear he didn't think his dad was guilty. He didn't come right out and say it. "Hard to believe your dad did what they said he did," was the way he put it. That was all Nick needed to hear. The way he saw it, there were two kinds of people in the world. Those who believed his father was innocent, and those who didn't. And you wouldn't need a very large room to accommodate everyone in the first group.

Al arrived, looking naked without his Bluetooth. At exactly 9:30, Pete pushed a buzzer and the door slid open.

The visiting room was about as cold and unwelcoming as a room could possibly be. It was furnished with a dozen plastic tables, each surrounded by four plastic chairs. A longer table with a few magazines, a deck of playing cards, and some children's coloring books sat in front of one wall. A few vending machines were lined up against another.

Only one table was free. Nick sat down while Al went over and leafed through the pile of magazines. A woman with big hair was seated at the next table, across from a young guy with a snake tattooed on his neck.

"I wish you could understand," the woman whispered.

"Don't do this to me, babe. I need you. You're all that keeps me going." Her boyfriend stroked her arm. "I love you."

"I love you, too," she said. "But I can't do this anymore. I'm twenty-three. I'll be thirty-seven when you get out. I can't … I just can't." The man with the snake tattoo turned away from her and stared at the wall. "Try to understand," she pleaded.

He wheeled around. "You want my blessing?" He spat the words at her. "Well you're not going to get it!"

"Don't be like this," she said.

"Get the hell out of here!" She stood up and put her hand on his cheek. He slapped it away and got to his feet. He stared at her with a stone-cold expression on his face, then walked to the door that led back to the cells. The woman watched him leave, but he didn't look back at her. He pushed the buzzer on the wall beside the door. It slid open and he disappeared through it. The woman walked out of the visiting room, tears streaming down her face.

Just then Al came over to the table with a copy of Sports Illustrated. "This is the most recent issue they've got," he said, pointing to the cover picture of Indianapolis quarterback Mickey Payton, celebrating the Colts' Super Bowl victory three years earlier. "I guess time doesn't mean too much in here." He sat down and started reading.

A minute or so later, Nick's father arrived. As soon as he saw Nick his face broke into a big smile. It seemed to Nick that there was more grey in his father's hair than there had been the last time. His dad wrapped him in a big embrace, and then shook hands with Al.

"You look good, big guy," Al said. "How are you doing?"

"I'm good. How was the drive?"

"There was nobody on the road," Nick said.

"They heard Nick was driving," Al joked. "Helen got you the books you wanted. We put them in the mail this morning. You should get them in a few days."

"Thank her for me," Nick's dad said. "Got a joke for you."

"I can't wait," Al said sarcastically. He knew what was coming.

"So this guy needs a heart transplant. His doctor tells him two hearts are available: one is from a twenty-five year-old marathon runner, the other belonged to a sixty-five year-old agent who smoked three packs of cigarettes a day. The patient chooses the agent's heart. "Why that one?" the doctor asks. "Because I want one that's never been used." Nick's dad laughed. He always laughed at his own jokes.

"Your dad's a funny guy," Al said to Nick.

"Is there anything we need to talk about?" his dad asked Al when he stopped laughing.

"We're good. You guys go outside. I'll catch up on my reading," Al said, waving his magazine.

"Okay if we go to the bullpen, Karl?" Nick's dad asked one of the guards. Karl nodded.

They walked out the door at the far end of the visiting room, and into a rectangular courtyard surrounded on three sides by a high brick wall. It was a nasty day, cold and raw, but this was the only place where they could have some privacy—as long as they ignored the two guards and the video cameras mounted on top of the brick walls. It was okay for them to be alone out here, but if they had stayed inside, Al would have had to sit at the same table with them. You could go crazy trying to understand the point of that rule, which was probably why they made it.

Nick's father looked up at the grey sky. "Let's hope the rain holds off," he said. The beginning of a visit was always awkward. It was impossible to forget where they were, but they both did their best to pretend everything was normal. Anything else only made it worse. "You look thin, son. Have you lost weight?"

"I don't think so. Did you get the photo?" Nick asked. Suddenly he felt absolutely certain that Baldy Number Six was the guy they were looking for. He had the same feeling he sometimes had the moment before he scored a goal. The puck would still be on his stick but he could already see it in the net.

"I did," his dad said. "It's not him."

Nick felt like he'd been kicked in the gut. "Are you sure?" he asked. "Did you see the earring? Maybe that's what you forgot."

"The man I saw didn't have an earring. Look, Nick. We need to talk." His dad's serious expression made Nick very nervous. "I don't want you looking for this guy anymore."

"What do you mean? We have to find him so you can get out of here."

"I had the best private detectives in the city on the case for more than a year, and they came up empty."

"I'll find him, Dad. I will. I know I will." Nick could hear the panic in his voice.

"We don't even know if this guy is in Vancouver."

"We don't know he isn't."

"Let's face it, Nick. It will take a miracle to find him."

"Miracles happen."

His dad sighed heavily. "What this has done to my life is bad enough. I don't want to see it ruin yours."

"Is this about school? I know my marks have dropped but that's no big deal. I'll study harder. I promise."

"It's not just about your marks, although that does concern me. You need to get your act together or you're not going to get into university. That may not seem important to you now ..."

"It means sweet you-know-what," Nick said angrily.

His father sighed again. He had always stressed the importance of Nick getting a university education. School came first, ahead of hockey and everything else. Even when he had been on the road with the Canucks, he would call every day to make sure Nick had done his homework.

"I'm worried about you, Nick. You're not playing hockey, you stopped seeing Sherry, you don't hang out with your friends anymore."

"You want me to start playing hockey again? Fine. I'll start playing again. You want me to hang out with the guys. Fine. I'll hang out with the guys." As for seeing Sherry, well, there wasn't much he could do about that.

"That's not the point," his father said. "You can't put your life on hold waiting for something that might never happen. I know you're doing it for me, and I love you for it, but I don't want you throwing your life away for me. All that's going to do is make both of us miserable."

"So you're just going to give up?" Nick shouted. One of the guards looked in their direction. "Winners never quit and quitters never win. Isn't that what you always told me? Well you can give up if you want but I'm not going to." He stared at his father belligerently.

His dad looked at him gently. "When I first came here, I was angry all the time. I woke up angry and I went to bed angry. I couldn't sleep because I was so angry. I didn't talk to anybody. I didn't have any friends. All I had was my anger. I had every right to be angry; I didn't kill Marty Albertson, and I shouldn't be in prison. Then I realized I had to make a choice. I could stay angry for the rest of my life, but that wouldn't get me out of here, it would only make me a bitter human being. Or I could accept the cards I've been dealt and get on with my life as best I could. That's what I've decided to do. And that's what you have to do too. You need to understand that I'm going to be here for a long, long time and there is nothing—nothing—either of us can do about it."

His dad put his hands on Nick's shoulders. "Life is short, and you only get to go around once. You want to do something for me? Go out there and live it to the fullest."

Nick could feel his lips quivering. *Please don't let me cry,* he prayed. There must be something his father could do. His whole life, no matter what the problem was, even when his mom died, as terrible as that had been, Nick had always felt safe. He knew his dad would take care of everything. Even after he went to jail, Nick never doubted that things would turn out all right, that it wouldn't be long before the two of them were together again.

"I can't live without you, Dad. I just can't." His father didn't say anything; this time he didn't have an answer. Nick could see he was near tears himself.

For the first time in his life, Nick didn't feel safe.

Nick felt the anger at his dad rise up as he and Al walked toward the parking lot. *How could he just give up like that?*

"You okay?" Al asked.

"Yeah."

"I know it's none of my business, but Steve's right.

You can't spend the rest of your life running around on a wild goose chase."

"Whatever." So Al knew what his dad had told him. He should have guessed. His father would want Al to tell him if Nick was out there doing what he wasn't supposed to do. And it was no surprise that Al agreed with him. Al had made it clear from the start that he thought Nick was wasting his time looking for Baldy. He remembered how Al reacted when he showed him the photo of Baldy Number One. He had barely looked at the picture. "Do yourself a favor, Nick," he had said. "Don't drive yourself crazy looking for this guy. If Cuthbert"—the detective his dad had hired— "couldn't find him, you sure as hell aren't going to." Nick didn't bother showing Al any photos after that.

"You going to be okay with this?" Al asked.

"Sure. No problem." Al gave him a searching look, then turned on his cellphone and punched in a few numbers. "Dude ..." he said into the phone.

Nick's mind was as foggy as the weather on the drive back to Vancouver. His stomach was in knots. He tried to make sense of what had happened back at the prison. *What am I supposed to do now? Just go on with the rest of my life as if nothing has happened? As if Dad isn't in prison for a crime he didn't commit?*

His father wouldn't even be eligible for parole for twenty-five years. Make that twenty-four years, since he'd almost served a year now. Even if he got out then—and there were no guarantees—Nick would be forty-one years old; older than his dad was now. And his father would be sixty-two. An old man.

One time when he was at the prison, a woman was at the next table with her four-year-old son. The boy was sitting beside her when a few prisoners came into the visiting room at the same time. "Go give daddy a hug," the woman told him. The little boy burst into tears. He didn't know which man was his father.

Nick imagined himself, ten or fifteen years down the road, coming to the prison with his kid. "Go give grandpa a hug." *Screw that,* he thought. He didn't care what his dad told him, he wasn't going to stop looking for Baldy. He just wouldn't tell him about it. His father wanted him to play hockey and get his grades up? Not a problem. But he could get straight A's and lead the Lightning to the Stanley Cup, and as long as his father was behind bars, it wouldn't change a goddamn thing. There was only one way to do that; get his dad out of jail. And that's what he was going to do. The knot in his stomach eased. A feeling of relief washed over him.

"Take the next exit," Al said as they approached Abbotsford. "I gotta take a leak."

Nick nodded. He signaled, turned off the highway, and pulled in at the first gas station. Al got out of the car, then turned back and looked at Nick through the open door.

"Don't make the mistake of thinking your dad's a quitter," he said. "It took a lot more courage for him to face up to his situation than to try to deny it. You want to make it easier on him? Get out there and make him proud of you."

Oh I will, Nick thought. *I will.*

CHAPTER EIGHT

Two days later Nick was sitting in the main office, reading over his English assignment while he waited to see McAndrew.

"*Do Not Go Gentle into that Good Night*," he had written, "is a poem about dealing with death. The poet, Dylan Thomas, tells us that we should not accept death easily, we should fight against it to the end. The message of the poem can be found in the first three lines: *Do not go gentle into that good night,/Old age should burn and rave at close of day;/Rage, rage against the dying of the light.*"

The first time Nick read the poem, it made him think of his dad's situation. His father wasn't dying, at least not literally, but he was trapped in a kind of living death, wasn't he?

He continued reading. "The poem is about death, but its message can also be applied to other situations in our lives where we are faced with things that seem to be beyond our control. When that happens we have a choice. We can either 'go gently'—be a quitter who gives up and throws in the towel—or we can 'rage, rage,'—refuse to give up and fight with all our strength."

Nick recalled what his dad had told him at the prison. "I have to get on with my life the best I can." *I know Dad can't be raging all the time,* Nick thought, *but he's going a little too gently for my taste.*

40

"Mr. McAndrew will see you now," said Mrs. Lewis. This was the first year ever that Nick had known one of the school secretaries by name, but that's what happened when you needed a late slip as often as he did.

Nick knocked on the VP's door. "Come in."

McAndrew was working at his computer. He glanced up. "Be right with you." He pointed to a chair, then turned back to his computer.

Nick sat down. He stared at the strands of red hair pasted across McAndrew's scalp. *Give it up, bud,* he thought, *the comb-over just isn't working.* Hard to believe he once had a full head of hair, but the proof was there in the framed picture on his desk—McAndrew at seventeen or eighteen, in his Kingston Frontenac hockey uniform, smiling for the camera. According to Charlie Boyle, the Lightning's assistant coach, McAndrew had been a promising junior who had a chance of making it to the NHL—until he was in a car accident that ended his career and left him with a permanent limp.

Nick looked at the picture on the wall behind the desk, a photo of a plate of bacon and eggs with the caption: THE CHICKEN MADE THE CONTRIBUTION. THE PIG MADE THE COMMITMENT. The team had given it to McAndrew for his birthday the year before. It pretty much summed up his coaching philosophy. Nick knew he'd have to convince McAndrew he was ready to make the commitment if he was going to get back on the team.

A couple of minutes passed while McAndrew tapped away on his keyboard. Nick took a few deep breaths, remembering the advice the guys had given him when they talked about it the day before.

They were all sitting in Google's kitchen, except for Biggie, who was working at his father's clothing store.

Nick's friends were positive McAndrew would let him back on the team, but Nick wasn't so sure.

"The rules say you've got to go to the tryouts if you want to be on the team," he pointed out.

"McAndrew can do whatever he wants," Ivan said. "He doesn't care about the rules."

"I know," Nick said, "but he's a hard-ass."

"He's a hard-ass who hates losing," Google said.

"He's going to make you sweat, but he'll take you back," Ivan predicted. "Whatever he says, you've just got to sit there and take it."

"Can I have another helping of that yummy shit, Coach?" was the way Red put it.

"What can I do for you, Nick?" McAndrew asked, turning away from the computer at last.

Oh, I just came here to shoot the shit 'cause you and I are such good friends. "I want to rejoin the team," Nick said.

McAndrew leaned back in his chair. He gave Nick a searching look that seemed to last forever. *Damn,* Nick thought, as he looked the coach in the eye. *He's not going to let me play.*

"I have to tell you I'm reluctant to put you back on the team," McAndrew finally said. "Very reluctant."

Nick breathed a sigh of relief. If McAndrew wasn't going to let him back on the team, all he had to say was that it wouldn't be fair to the players who attended the tryouts. But he didn't. He just wanted to make Nick sweat a little, like Ivan said. Nick nodded somberly.

"If you had come in here at the start of the season, I wouldn't have had a problem. But why now? What's changed?"

"I wasn't ready then. I'm ready now." It wasn't much

of an explanation, but Nick didn't feel like talking about his father with McAndrew.

"I know you left the team last year because of your situation," McAndrew said. The *situation*. Nick wished he could rip the frigging word right out of the dictionary. "I don't want to sound unsympathetic," McAndrew continued, "but that hasn't changed. How do I know you won't come back in a month and tell me you don't feel like playing after all?"

"I wouldn't be here if I wasn't a hundred per cent sure," Nick said, keeping his gaze steady. *Can I have another helping of that yummy shit, Coach?*

"I won't pretend we couldn't use you," McAndrew said, "but I've got more than the team to think about. I'm an educator as well as a coach. You say you can commit to the team. Fine. But you're also going to have to commit to your studies."

"I intend to," Nick said, "whether I'm back on the team or not." *That was a nice touch,* he thought. The grilling reminded him of a scene near the end of *Cool Hand Luke,* one of his dad's choices for movie night.

In the movie Luke, played by Paul Newman, keeps escaping from prison but he keeps getting caught. After he's captured a third time, the guards beat the crap out of him until he can't move. Luke lies there in the dirt, begging the guards not to hit him again. "You got your mind right, Luke?" the head guard asks. "I got it right, boss. I got it right."

McAndrew continued studying Nick's face. *You got your mind right, Nick?*

Nick didn't blink. *I got it right, boss. I got it right.*

The two locked eyes for a few more seconds. Then McAndrew nodded. "Okay," he said. "See you at practice tomorrow."

Ivan was waiting in the hallway when Nick came out of the office. "Well?" he asked.

"He said no."

Ivan sagged. "You've got to be joking," he said.

"I am," Nick said.

"Prick," Ivan said. A smile spread across his face. Then he punched Nick in the shoulder. "I told you he'd say yes."

McAndrew hadn't given Nick an unconditional yes. He was on probation. He had to get a 75% average on his Christmas exams in order to stay on the team. "That's what you'll need to get into a decent university," the coach said. Apparently he took his responsibilities as an educator more seriously than Nick thought.

"Did he give you a hard time?" Ivan asked, as they walked to English class.

"Not as hard as he would have if you guys weren't one and four."

"Man, I am so looking forward to playing with you again," Ivan said. The two of them, along with Red, had always played on the same line. At every level—Atom, Peewee, Bantam, and now Midget—Ivan had always been one of the top scorers in the league, but he'd been struggling ever since Nick stopped playing.

"McAndrew's old school. He's not going to put us back together right away," Nick said. "Especially since our next two games are against Chilliwack and Langley."

Chilliwack and Langley were the two weakest teams in the league. The Lightning were playing both of them in the coming week, and as badly as they were playing, they would have to completely fall apart to lose either game.

"I hope he doesn't wait too long," Ivan muttered as

they walked to class.

"Everybody goes through slumps, dude," Nick said. "Look at Melanson. One goal in his first fourteen games last year. And he ended up with forty-seven. Don't worry. You'll snap out of it."

"I know," Ivan said, cheering up.

"Hand in your assignments before you sit down," Putnam said when they entered the classroom. Nick opened his knapsack, took out his paper on the Dylan Thomas poem, and put it on Putnam's desk. Sherry was standing behind him.

"Hey," he said.

"Hey," she answered.

"How you doing?"

"Good. You?"

"Good."

Sherry added her assignment to the pile on Putnam's desk and took her seat. Nick walked past her desk on the way to his own. She didn't look up.

It wasn't much, Nick thought, but it was the longest conversation they'd had in a long, long time.

CHAPTER NINE

Nick spent most of the class looking at the back of Sherry's head, hoping she'd turn around and acknowledge him. She didn't. When the bell rang, she grabbed her bag and walked out of the classroom without a backward glance.

Nick went straight home, hit the books for a couple of hours, and then called Google. "Al's going to drop me off at your house at six o'clock," he said. "That gives us an hour to make it to the game."

"What did you tell him we were doing?" Google asked.

"I said we were working on an assignment."

There was no assignment. Nick and Google were going to the Vancouver Giants hockey game, not because the Giants were good—they sucked big time—but because they hoped Baldy would be there. They went to hockey games all over the city. It was Google's idea. He pointed out that since everything about the case was connected to hockey, there was a good chance that Baldy was a hockey fan. They went to a lot of Canucks games too. Well, sort of went. Nick was so angry with the team for the way it had treated his dad that he refused to watch them play. He and Google would show up at the arena a half-hour before the game to look for Baldy and then leave after it started.

"What subject did you say the assignment was for?" Google asked.

"He didn't ask and I didn't say."

"Let's say it's math, in case he does. Got to keep our story straight."

"Okay," Nick said. It was a good idea. He knew Al wouldn't ask him but Helen might.

Google had asked only one question when Nick told him that he was going to keep looking for Baldy, even though he wasn't supposed to: "How will we know we've found him if we can't show his picture to your dad?"

Nick had already thought about that. "We're going to have to wait until I can prove that I've got my shit together. If I'm doing well in school and playing hockey, he won't be able to tell me that looking for Baldy is ruining my life."

"How long is that going to take?" Google asked.

"Until we get our report cards."

"Then you better start hitting the books," Google said.

He had that right. They would get their report cards just before the winter holidays. That was about six weeks from now, a long time for an innocent man to sit in a prison cell, but a short time for Nick to catch up on all the schoolwork he'd ignored for the past two months.

Nick walked into Al's office. Al was on the phone, his back to the door. "I'll see you at eight-thirty … "Yeah, I got it!" he said in a pissed off voice and hung up. Nick could see the angry look on Al's face in the mirror behind his desk. Al glanced into the mirror and saw Nick watching him. He swiveled around in his chair. "Clients," he said, shaking his head in disgust. "If I could get rid of them, this job would be a piece of cake … Ready?"

Nick and Al went downstairs. Helen was sitting on the couch in the living room. "See you later, sweetie," Al said. He bent down and kissed her on the cheek.

"Maybe you can pick Nick up at Google's on your way home from the meeting," Helen suggested. Al was going to a meeting with Gambler's Anonymous, an organization for people who were addicted to gambling.

"Sure. It should be over around nine," Al said.

"We probably won't be done the assignment by then," Nick said, "but I'll call you if we are."

"Okay," said Helen. "Don't forget it's a school night." She turned to Al. "You better get going. You don't want to be late."

"Yes dear," he said good-humoredly.

Al had always gambled—that was no secret—but a few years ago things got completely out of control. Nick's dad told him that Al owed his bookie so much money that he nearly lost the house. Helen was so upset that she threatened to leave him unless he joined GA. Al signed up the next day and he'd been going to their weekly meetings ever since. He wasn't about to lose Helen. "She's the best thing that ever happened to me," he was fond of saying to anyone who'd listen. He meant it too. All you had to do was see the way he looked at her to know that.

Nick stood just outside the gate, peering at the faces of the fans as they filed out of the Pacific Coliseum, grumbling about the Giants' fourth loss in a row. Google was at another gate, doing the same thing.

They were looking for the bald man they had seen during the second intermission. He had been going up the escalator as they were going down. Nick only got a quick glimpse as he went by, but he fit the general description of the man they were looking for so he snapped a photo with his cellphone as they passed. Nick had tried to see if the guy limped as he got off the escalator, but the crowd was so thick it had been impossible to tell.

As soon as he disappeared, Nick and Google had

checked out the photo.

"Look!" Google had said in an excited voice. "He doesn't have any eyebrows. That could be the thing your dad forgot."

Nick took a look. He hadn't noticed the missing eyebrows when he took the picture. All he'd seen was the bald head. Google was right. This was something his father might not have remembered. But Nick had been down this road too often to get wound up about it. "Doesn't mean jack shit, unless he has a limp," he said.

The Kootenay Ice players were coming through the gate. They were laughing and joking, just as you'd expect from a team that had waltzed to a 5–1 victory. They looked a lot bigger in person than they did on the ice. A couple of kids ran up to one of the Kootenay players, and asked for his autograph. Nick recognized Jake "the Snake" Chambers, the team's star player and a sure-fire first round pick in the upcoming NHL draft. Chambers walked by the kids without breaking stride. *What a prick,* Nick thought. He remembered the time his dad tore a strip off a Canucks' rookie who did what Chambers had just done. "It would have taken you two seconds to give that kid your autograph," his father had said. "And he would have remembered it for the rest of his life."

Nick turned his gaze back toward the exit. A skinny bald man was standing on the other side of the gate, his back to Nick. Nick wondered if it was the guy with no eyebrows. He started walking toward him when he spotted Al Hawkins approaching from the other direction. Nick ducked behind a pillar. He hoped Al hadn't seen him. Nick's dad knew that he had been coming to the Giants games in search of Baldy. If Al told him that he'd seen Nick at the game, his dad would know Nick was disobeying him. Nick didn't want to think about would happen then.

Wait a minute, Nick thought. *What's Al doing here? He's supposed to be at his GA meeting.*

Just then Al stopped in front of the bald man. They nodded at each other, the kind of nod you give to somebody you expect to see, not to someone you just bumped into.

I bet that's the guy Al was talking to in his office, Nick thought. They were going to meet at eight-thirty. Nick checked his watch. It was 8:35. He remembered that Al told him the caller was one of his clients. *Bullshit.* Nick didn't know who the man was, but he knew one thing for sure. This guy was not one of Al's clients. No way he was a professional hockey player, not with that scrawny body.

Al took an envelope from his jacket pocket and handed it to the bald man. He opened it, took out a wad of bills, and thumbed through them. *Oh my God!* A crazy thought rushed into Nick's mind. *It's Baldy. Al's paying him off.* A combination of horror and excitement flowed through Nick's body. The bald man put the money back in the envelope and slipped it inside his jacket. He and Al nodded to each other again, then Al marched away.

Nick kept his eye on the bald man, determined not to let him out of his sight. His heart was beating wildly. His mind was racing. The man took out a cigarette and put it in his mouth. Then he walked away, walking without the slightest trace of a limp. It wasn't Baldy.

It didn't take Nick long to figure out what was going on. It had nothing to do with Albertson's murder. Al was gambling again. And judging by the stack of bills he'd handed over, he wasn't just betting lunch money.

I can't believe it, Nick said to himself. *If Helen finds out, the shit is really going to hit the fan.*

CHAPTER TEN

The next day Nick and Google got to the arena early so Nick could pick up his equipment before practice. Google laid it out on the bench. Neck guard, shoulder pads, elbow pads, shin pads, gloves, pants, socks, helmet. Then Google handed Nick a jersey. "I've been saving this for you," he said. Number 77. Nick had started using his dad's number when he was playing Atom, and he'd been using it ever since.

"Thanks, bud."

The other players started to filter into the locker room. One by one they came over and welcomed him back onto the team.

"Great to have you back."

"Good to see you in uniform again, Nick."

"We really missed you, man."

"Either somebody shit in their hockey bag," Red said as he walked in, sniffing the air, "or Macklin's back on the team." Everybody laughed. Red came over to Nick, and high-fived him. "About frigging time," he said.

"Guess we got the championship all locked up now," a tall dark-haired guy said sarcastically to a huge guy with a shaved head standing beside him.

"I got something for you, Kenny," Red said. He put his hand in his pocket, dug around as if he was looking for something, then pulled his hand out and gave Kenny the finger.

So that's Kenny Lipton, Nick said to himself as he strapped on his shoulder pads. He'd heard all about him. Lipton was leading the Lightning in scoring but everybody—even Ivan who never had a bad word to say about anybody—said he was a selfish player who cared only about his personal statistics. The big guy had to be Josh Parry, another newcomer to the team. Nick had heard about him too. He was a good defenseman with a wicked shot, and, according to Google, a world-class dick.

Suddenly, a pair of arms wrapped Nick in a huge bear hug from behind. "Don't I know you from somewhere?" Biggie said. Nick squirmed to get free, but Biggie wasn't ready to let him go.

"Aren't you going to kiss him first?" Parry asked. Lipton laughed. So did a few of the other players. Biggie put Nick down and glared at Josh who glared right back. It was clear there was no love lost between the two of them. Google caught Nick's eye from across the room. He had been complaining about Lipton and Parry ever since the season started. *"See what I mean?"* the look said.

A piercing whistle got everybody's attention. The assistant coach, Charlie Boyle, stood by the door. "Three minutes. Let's get a move on."

McAndrew blew his whistle. "Bring it in," he bellowed, as he skated to center ice, dragging his bum leg behind him. Nick was never so glad in his life for a practice to end. His lungs felt like they were going to explode and every muscle in his body was screaming. He knew he was out of shape, but he had no idea it was this bad. *I shouldn't be surprised,* he thought. *That's what six months without breaking a sweat will do to you.*

He joined the rest of the players in a semi-circle around McAndrew. "Game time tomorrow is seven, so I want everyone here by six. Get a good night's rest. I don't want anybody thinking we can take a win for granted. We haven't earned the right, not with the way we've been playing."

He put his stick out in front of him. The players did likewise. "One ... " he started. The players joined in.

"Two ... Three ... Lightning!"

Nick joined the line of players filing off the ice. "Hold on, Macklin," McAndrew barked. "You're not done."

Ivan tapped him on his shin pads with his hockey stick as he skated by him. "Hang in there," he said, with a sympathetic smile.

"You poor bastard," said Red.

Nick skated over to McAndrew. "Set up the pylons," he said. "Let's see if we can work off some of that rust."

Nick placed the rubber cones along the length of the ice. For the first fifteen minutes, McAndrew put him through a series of drills that had him weaving around the pylons until his legs felt like they each weighed a ton. The next fifteen minutes were dedicated to pure conditioning, a variety of stop-and-start exercises that left Nick gasping for breath. Just when he thought he couldn't take another step, McAndrew blew his whistle and motioned for him to come over. "How do you feel?" he asked.

"Never better," Nick said with a smile.

"Glad to hear it," McAndrew said. He started skating toward one end of the rink. After a few strides he turned and looked at Nick, who was still standing at center ice. "What are you waiting for?" he asked.

Oh, shit, Nick thought. He had a sneaking suspicion he knew what was next on the agenda.

He was right. They didn't call it the Suicide Drill for nothing. Skate from the goal line to the blue line and back. Do one push-up. Skate to the center line and back. Two push-ups. The other blue line and back. Three push-ups. Sprint the length of the ice to the goal line. Four push-ups. Then do it again in the other direction until you were back at the starting point. Repeat the drill—twice more—once with power crunches instead of push-ups, and a second time with burpees. A total of twenty push-ups, twenty crunches, twenty burpees and close to a mile of skating.

McAndrew blew his whistle. Nick dug his blades into the ice and took off. Two Suicide Drills later, it took every ounce of strength he had to make it to his feet after the last burpee.

"How do you feel?" McAndrew asked.

"Never better," Nick said. Then he bent over and puked his guts out.

McAndrew waited until he stopped heaving. "Seven a.m. tomorrow."

CHAPTER ELEVEN

The next day Nick got off the bus in front of the school. He had never been so stiff in his life. It had been a major accomplishment just to drag himself out of bed in the morning, let alone get to the rink for his seven o'clock workout with McAndrew. He had to stretch for five minutes before he could even lace up his skates. Then McAndrew put him through his paces for a solid hour. Muscles he didn't know he had were hurting.

McAndrew was waiting at the top of the steps by the front door. Nick forced himself to stand straight and quicken his stride. He took the stairs two at a time. "Morning, Coach," he said with a smile.

"Morning, Nick," McAndrew answered. "How are you feeling?"

"Never better."

"Have a good day."

"You too," Nick said, as he bounced past him. He continued down the hall and walked into English class, slowing down as soon as he was out of McAndrew's line of sight. He carefully eased himself into his seat.

Ivan shook his head. "You look like an old man," he said.

"I feel like an old man."

"You going to be able to play tonight?"

"Once I get going I'll be okay. Not that it matters.

McAndrew said he was only going to give me a couple of shifts."

"You're going to have to earn your way back into the lineup," the coach told Nick after that morning's workout. It wasn't what Nick wanted to hear, but at least he knew where things stood. His dad always said the best coaches were the ones who communicated with their players. McAndrew might not have been cutting him any slack, but Nick had to admit he was a straight shooter. He understood how players felt, because he'd played at a high level himself. Funny how McAndrew never talked about his playing days. Nick figured it must still hurt the coach to know his chance of making it to the NHL had been ended by something as a random as a car accident.

Putnam strolled down the aisle, handing back the Dylan Thomas assignment. He smiled as he gave Nick his paper. "Good work," Putnam said. Nick's mark was written at the top of the page: an A. McAndrew would be pleased. So would his dad.

"All right!" Fred Feldman shouted. "D plus." He triumphantly waved his assignment in the air.

"You the man," yelled Donnie Keagan. Fred leaned over, put his right elbow on his knee, rested his chin in his hand, and pretended to be deep in thought, mimicking the pose of a famous statue called *The Thinker.*

Putnam didn't miss a beat. "You flatter yourself," he said. The class laughed.

"*Most* of you," Putnam said, looking pointedly at Fred, "understood that the poem explores our feelings in the face of death. When Dylan Thomas wrote the poem, his father, to whom he was very close, was dying. So what does he mean in the final stanza when he says, 'Curse, bless me now with your fierce tears, I pray'?"

Emma Jenkins, the class suck, waved her hand in the air.

Nick didn't hear her answer. He was thinking about *his* father. He wished he would do a little more cursing, and a little less meditating.

They had spoken on the telephone the night before. For the first time ever Nick's dad hadn't said a word about his case, and Nick didn't dare bring it up. Instead, he had to listen to his father tell him that he was going to apply for a transfer to a prison closer to Vancouver. As if that was going to make a difference.

Gail Porter raised her hand. Putnam nodded at her. "We're all going to die, so I think it's better to accept it and try to come to terms with it."

"Dying sucks," said Jason Turner. "If I was God, nobody would die."

"If you were God," said Zoe Taylor, "we'd be listening to heavy metal twenty-four seven." Everybody laughed.

"The fact that we die proves there is no God," said Jody Davis.

"Yeah, if there was a God, nobody would have cancer. And everybody would have a home and enough to eat," added Laura McNeil.

And my mom wouldn't have died and my dad wouldn't be in jail, Nick thought.

It was hard to believe it had been almost seven years since his mother died. At first Nick didn't think the pain would ever go away, but after a while—a long while—it did. Or mostly did. Every so often, without any warning, a wave of sadness would wash over him. He and his dad always went to the cemetery on the anniversary of her death. Even after all this time, when he read the words carved on her tombstone—ELIZABETH MACKLIN, BELOVED MOTHER AND WIFE—the pain came rushing back. It was bittersweet. As much as it hurt, it kept his mom alive in his memory. The worst thing would be to feel nothing at all. His dad always put a single yellow rose on her grave. "Yellow was her favorite color, remember?" he would say. Nick would nod, but the truth was he didn't know if he actually remembered it himself, or if he was just remembering what his father had told him.

"We're not done with Dylan Thomas," Putnam said, as the class came to an end. "Your assignment is to imagine the conversation he had with his father when his father was on his deathbed. Mr. Feldman, you'll be delighted to hear that it can be as short as you want."

"I can do it in one sentence," Fred said. "Hey pops, where's your will?" The bell rang as the class erupted in laughter.

"I hate to end on such a thought-provoking note," Putnam said, "but unfortunately we've run out of time."

Nick had to push off his desk with both hands in order to get to his feet. "That's pathetic, dude," Ivan said. Nick shrugged and put his books in his knapsack.

Putnam stopped him as he and Ivan walked past his desk. "Got a minute, Nick?" he asked.

"Catch you later," Ivan said, as he left the classroom.

"Mr. McAndrew told me about your conversation," Putnam said. "If you need any help getting up to speed, just let me know."

"Thanks." Nick waited for Putnam to say that he was happy Nick was playing hockey again, the way everybody else had. They all seemed to think it meant that he'd turned the corner, that he had finally accepted the *situation*. They didn't know shit.

"No problem," Putnam said. "Keep up the good work."

Sherry was putting her books away when he walked by her locker.

"Hey."

"Hey. I hear you're playing hockey again," she said, looking up at him. Her eyes were green, but in this light they looked blue.

"Yeah."

"That's good," she said. Somehow, coming from her, it didn't piss him off.

"Yeah. Got my first game tonight." His heart was beating a mile a minute. She's so beautiful, he thought. Whenever he told her how beautiful she was—and he used to tell her a lot—she would beam, as if it was the first time he'd ever said it. Nick asked her about it once. "Don't you get tired of hearing how beautiful you are?" "You don't know much about women, do you?" she answered.

Sherry closed her locker. She was wearing a T-shirt that said REAL MEN BEAT EGGS. It was stretched tight across her breasts. He tried not to stare.

"I gotta run," she said. "See you later. Good luck tonight."

"Thanks."

He watched her as she walked away. She stopped halfway down the hall and turned around. "Hey Nick," she called out. "Play the man, not the puck." Nick laughed. Sherry waved, and then headed off.

Play the man, not the puck. He knew she had no idea what that meant. She just liked the sound of it. Sherry wasn't interested in hockey or in any sport for that matter. She used to say that all sports were the same, the players just wore different costumes. Not uniforms. Costumes. He chuckled just thinking about it.

The first time Sherry met his dad—it was after one of Nick's games—he asked her what she thought of Nick's play. "He's got to learn how to play the man, not the puck," she said solemnly. Cracked his dad right up. "She's a keeper," he said to Nick later.

Good advice, Nick thought. *Too bad I didn't take it.* He watched Sherry until she got to the end of the corridor and disappeared around the corner. He wondered if she was on her way to meet Joe College.

CHAPTER TWELVE

"What's the matter, Nick? You don't like my cooking anymore?" Red's father, Carmen Rizzuto, surveyed Nick's barely touched plate of spaghetti Bolognese with a sad look on his face. He took it personally when his customers didn't polish off the food he prepared.

"It's great, Mr. Rizzuto," Nick said. Even though he knew he wasn't going to get much ice time, he was too nervous about playing again to eat.

"Eat," Carmen ordered. "You need energy for the game."

"Leave the boy alone and get back in the kitchen. The fish was just delivered." Carmen's wife, Angelina, put her hands on her husband's shoulders and steered him to the kitchen. She had banned him from the dining area not long after La Fortuna opened because he kept getting angry at customers who left food on their plates.

"When I was a boy, my father would beat us if we didn't finish every scrap," Carmen muttered.

"Stop making up stories. Your father never laid a hand on you. He should have, but he didn't." Angelina rolled her eyes. "Go! Use your imagination on the sea bass," she said. She turned to the table. "More spaghetti, Arnold?" Arnold was Biggie's given name. Angelina was the only one who could get away with using it.

"Yes, please," he said, holding up his plate. Angelina

spooned out a healthy portion.

"Giovanni," she said to her son—she never called him Red—"help me clear the table." Red piled plates halfway up his arm and followed his mother into the kitchen. Nick, Biggie, Google, and Ivan swiveled around in unison to watch Angelina walk away, hips swaying. Nick couldn't keep thoughts you shouldn't have about a friend's mother from crossing his mind.

"She's luscious," his mom had said after meeting Angelina for the first time. Nick's mother had been an English teacher. She was always using words nobody else used. "It means sexy," she told Nick when he asked. "In a nice way."

"Pass the milf," Ivan whispered. The other three burst out laughing. Red turned and glared at them, even though he couldn't possibly have heard. None of them, not even Biggie, would dare use the word *milf* in connection with Angela if Red was within hearing distance. He had a hair-trigger temper, and a comment about his mother would definitely pull the trigger. Of course, that didn't stop him from making crude comments about every girl who happened to cross his path. The fact that she might be some guy's sister never crossed his mind.

Biggie polished off his second helping of spaghetti. "You done with that?" he asked, pointing at Nick's plate.

"It's all yours ... Arnold," Nick said from his point of safety across the table. He slid his plate toward Biggie.

McAndrew didn't put Nick in the game until midway through the second period. The moment he stepped on the ice, he realized he had a long way to go before he'd be in game shape. He felt like he was skating in cement. Thirty seconds into his shift he was sucking wind, hoping he could hang on until the line change. He got two more shifts in the third period, but it was more of the same.

"I feel like this is the first time I ever played," Nick told Biggie as they filed off the ice at the end of the game.

"Don't get discouraged, dude," Biggie said. "It's only been a couple of days. Another week, and you'll be flying."

The Lightning won the game 6–1 but there was none of the post-game banter you'd normally hear after a victory. Beating the weakest team in the league wasn't cause for a major celebration but a win was still a win. Yet anybody who walked into the locker room would have thought the team had lost.

Ivan made his way around the room. "Good game. Good game," he said. He tapped each player on the shin pads with his stick, like he'd done after every game since he became team captain last year. Hardly anybody bothered to look up at him. *This isn't a team,* Nick thought. *It's just eighteen individuals who all happen to be wearing the same uniform.*

Ivan stopped in front of Kenny Lipton. It hadn't taken Nick long to see that Lipton's reputation as a selfish player was well deserved. He scored three of the Lightning's six goals and was a threat every time he touched the puck, but his defense was non-existent. "Good game, Kenny," Ivan said. "Good game."

"You too." Lipton said. "Keep shooting, man. They'll start to go in." It might have sounded like encouragement, but coming from Lipton, Nick knew it was a reminder that Ivan that had gone another game without scoring.

Ivan nodded and moved on. Lipton whispered something to Josh Parry, who was sitting beside him. Parry looked at Ivan and laughed.

Nick glanced at Google, who shook his head. *What did I tell you?*

Nick was dog-tired by the time he got back to the house. All he wanted to do was fall into bed, but he had three hours of studying ahead of him if he was going to be ready for the physics test on Friday. As he came through the front door, he heard Al and Helen talking in the kitchen. They weren't exactly talking: arguing was more like it.

"How long are you going to stay mad at me?" Al asked.

"You promised that you would go to *every* meeting."

"Once I learned that Jake Chambers' father was going to be at the game, I had to go or I would have lost any chance of landing the kid."

It took Nick a few seconds to figure out what was going on. Helen had found out that Al missed his GA meeting. And now he was trying to make her believe he'd gone to the Giants game to sign up Kootenay's star player, Jake "the Snake" Chambers.

"There's always a reason," Helen said.

"That's not fair, Helen. This is the first meeting I've missed in four years."

"I know," Helen said, her voice softening. "I guess I just can't forget how close we came to losing everything."

"I would never hurt you, sweetie. You know that. I love you."

"I love you too."

Nick wasn't surprised Helen bought Al's explanation. He sounded so convincing that if Nick hadn't seen Al hand an envelope of money to the guy at the Giants game, he would have believed it himself.

CHAPTER THIRTEEN

Nick stood in line to pay for his lunch. It was so loud in the cafeteria you could barely hear yourself think, but that was always the case on Fridays. Everybody was looking forward to the weekend. He was glad the physics test was over. He thought he'd done reasonably well, although there had been a couple of questions he couldn't answer.

After he got his change, Nick joined his friends at a table near the entrance. The five of them had sat there since the start of grade 9. Red laid claim to it a few days into their first term. "This way we can see the chicks coming and going," he explained.

They spent most of the lunch period talking about Kenny Lipton. "He doesn't care if we win as long as he gets his goals," Red said. "We're better off without him."

"He's the only guy on the team who's been putting the puck in the net," Ivan pointed out.

That's the truth, Nick thought. Lipton had scored half the team's goals so far this season.

"He's not half the player you are. Wait till McAndrew puts us back together with Nick," Red insisted.

"Ivan's the best. We all know that," Nick said. "But that doesn't mean we don't need Lipton. He's a big-time scorer, you can't deny that."

"I agree with Red. We're better off without him," said Google. "He's not a team player, and he never will be.

When's the last time he went into the corner like he wanted to come out with the puck? Doesn't McAndrew see that?"

"He sees it," said Biggie. "I'm tired of hearing you guys moan about Lipton. Can't you talk about anything else?"

"You bet," said Red. "Look at the rack on her," he said, pointing to a girl who had just come into the cafeteria. "Oh, Mama!"

"Aren't you ever going to grow up?" Biggie asked. Red only ever talked about two things: hockey and girls.

Sherry had never understood how Nick could be his friend. "He's a sexist pig," she said. "Tell me what you really think," Nick said. He tried to explain that Red was a true friend, someone he could count on to have his back, no matter what. He was fearless, too. He wouldn't back down for anybody. That made up for a lot of faults. "He's still a sexist pig," Sherry insisted.

"His heart's in the right place," Nick said. "He just needs to grow up."

That was more than three years ago, but Red still hadn't grown up.

Nick put his knapsack into his locker and took out his uniform. He had come to the arena straight from school, as he had all week, so he could cram in as much studying as possible before practice started. He couldn't waste a minute of his time if he was going to raise his marks up to where they needed to be. McAndrew had said he would need a 75 per cent average to stay on the team. He didn't know if the coach would hold him to it—everyone else just had to pass—but anything less, and his dad would never agree to let him keep looking for Baldy.

He put on his helmet and tightened the chinstrap. He walked down the hallway, stepped out onto the ice, and took a few warm-up laps around the rink, taking pleasure in the sound of his blades digging into the ice. For the first time since he rejoined the team, Nick was looking forward to practice. McAndrew had worked him hard all week. Sixty minutes in the morning and an extra thirty after practice every evening. The hard work had earned Nick a regular spot in the rotation. At yesterday's practice, McAndrew put him on the checking line with Paul Collins and John Armstrong. Their job was to stop the opposing team's best line from scoring. It wasn't glamorous, but it sure beat sitting on the bench.

Nick wasn't even breathing hard when the practice ended. He stepped off the ice and walked along the rubber carpet to the locker room. "You were flying out there," Google said, clapping a hand on his shoulder.

"Thanks. Felt good." McAndrew had pushed him to his limit, but he finally had his legs back. He was looking forward to the game against Langley, checking line or no checking line. He sat down on the bench in front of his locker to take off his equipment.

Charlie Boyle came into the locker room. "Good work, guys. Good work," he said. "The game is Sunday at noon. Don't be late."

Biggie let loose a huge fart. "Was that absolutely necessary?" Boyle asked.

"Yup," Biggie said. He never used two words when one would do.

"Make sure you get a good night's sleep."

Biggie farted again. He never used one word when none would do. The locker room filled with laughter. Even though the team was having its troubles, it was good to be back. Nick hadn't realized how much he'd missed it.

CHAPTER FOURTEEN

"I'm filing my application for a transfer tomorrow," Nick's dad said when he called Sunday morning. Nick and his dad spoke on the phone a few times a week. Prison rules about phone calls were actually pretty decent compared to the rules about everything else. Nick wasn't allowed to call in—if he wanted to talk to his dad, he had to leave a message—but his father could call out whenever he was free. "If the transfer's approved, I'll be sent to Mission or Abbotsford. Both are closer to Vancouver, so we'll be able to see more of each other."

"That's great, Dad," Nick said, trying to put a little enthusiasm in his voice. He couldn't believe his father was so excited about the transfer. Sure, he'd have more freedom in a medium security prison than he had in max, but jail was jail. He'd still be locked up.

"Everything okay at school?"

"Fine." Nick said. "I got an A on my English assignment."

"An A! That's fantastic," his dad said. "What was it on?"

"A poem by Dylan Thomas."

"Never heard of him. Who does he play for?" His dad laughed at his own joke. "How did the physics test go?"

"I think I did all right." Nick looked up as Al came into the kitchen. He pointed to his watch, indicating it was time to go. Nick nodded and Al left the kitchen.

"I have to go, Dad. Al is driving me to the game."

"Okay. I'll speak to you later. Good luck."

"Thanks." Nick hung up. He usually hated saying goodbye to his father, but today it was a relief. All his dad had wanted to talk about was the stupid transfer. Nick walked into the hall where Al was putting on his coat. Helen came downstairs.

"See you later," Al said.

"Don't forget to pick up the cake on your way home," Helen reminded him. Every Sunday night the Hawkins' children and grandchildren came over for a family dinner. Nick dreaded it. He got along with everybody, and they couldn't have been more welcoming, but, bottom line, it wasn't his family gathered around the dinner table. All it did was remind him of what he'd lost.

"Is it organic?" Al asked.

"Very funny," Helen said. "Call me after your GA meeting in case I need anything else," she added.

"Will do," Al said.

Where's he really going? Nick wondered.

The game went pretty much the way everyone expected. The Lightning trounced the hapless Langley Marauders, 8–1. The team played better than it did against Chilliwack, but they still had a way to go before they would give the best teams in the league a run for their money.

"You looked good out there, man," Biggie said to Nick when he came into the locker room.

"Thanks." Nick felt good about the way he'd played. He only had one assist to show for it, but he could have had three or four more if either of his line mates had a nose for the net. Nick watched Ivan walk around the room congratulating his teammates. "That's two in a row guys," he said. "We're on a roll." Ivan had gone another game without a goal. It was the longest scoring drought he'd ever suffered through, and Nick knew he was hurting inside, though you wouldn't know it from the way he was acting.

It reminded Nick of one of his dad's favorite life lessons. "Anybody can be happy when things are going well," he would say. "The real test of a person is how he handles adversity." Ivan was passing that test with flying colors, Nick thought, as he watched his friend make his rounds.

Nick sat down and began unlacing his skates. Kenny Lipton walked by without looking at him. Lipton had scored three of the Lightning's goals. It was his second hat trick in a row, but as usual, his defense left a lot to be desired.

"That last goal belongs on a highlight reel, dude," Josh Parry said, as Lipton sat down beside him. It was a beauty Nick had to admit. Lipton came down the ice one-on-one with the Langley defenseman, undressed him with a 360 degree spin, and snapped a wrist shot that beat the goalie high on his stick side.

"If he ever comes back on defense, *that* should go on a highlight reel," Red said to Nick in a voice loud enough for Lipton to hear. Lipton whispered something to Parry. Parry looked at Red and laughed. Red glared at him as Ivan walked up to Lipton and tapped him on the shin pads with his stick.

"Good game, Kenny," he said.

"Thanks. Once you get rolling, we're going to be tough to beat," Lipton said, just in case Ivan had forgotten he was in a slump.

"*If* he gets rolling," Parry added. Lipton snickered. Ivan

ignored the slight, but Red wasn't about to let it slide.

"There's more to hockey than scoring goals, douche bag," he said to Parry.

"Piss off."

"You're cute when you get mad," Red said, blowing an air kiss at Parry. Parry jumped to his feet but before things had a chance to go any further, McAndrew entered the locker room. From the scowl on his face you'd think the team had just lost 8–1.

"That was one sorry excuse for a hockey game," he said. "You guys play like that on Wednesday, and Surrey will kick your butts all the way to Timbuktu."

Just to make sure they got the message, McAndrew had Charlie Boyle take them to an exercise room on the second floor of the arena, where he led them through a brutal ninety-minute workout.

"Want to come over and watch the game?" Biggie asked, as they walked away from the arena. Staggered is more like it. Boyle had worked them to the limit.

"Can't. I got too much work to do," Nick said.

"The Seahawks are playing Oakland, dude," Red said. The Seattle Seahawks were their favorite NFL team. There was nothing Nick would have liked more than to kick back and watch the game with the guys, but between the two-a-days with McAndrew and catching up on the all the schoolwork he'd let slide since the start of the term, he hadn't looked for Baldy all week. School and hockey were eating up a lot of time, but finding Baldy was still Nick's top priority. He'd just have to figure out a way to do it all.

"I know. It sucks. But if I don't hit the books, I don't get to hit the ice." That ended the conversation. They all knew that Nick had dug himself a big hole by ignoring his studies for the first two months of the term.

Nick watched his friends pile into Biggie's car and take off. He trudged to the bus stop on the corner, holding his stick in one hand and towing his hockey bag with the other.

Nick's phone rang as the bus turned onto Georgia.

"Where the hell are you?" It was Al and he was pissed. *Shit,* Nick said to himself. He'd completely forgotten about Sunday night dinner. He looked at his watch. It was 6:15. He should have been at the house fifteen minutes ago.

"I'm at the library on Georgia," he said. "I lost track of the time." That last part was true, anyway. He couldn't believe he'd been on a bus for the past four hours. It had been a total waste of time. He'd seen plenty of bald men all right—it seemed like these days everyone shaved their heads as soon as they started losing a little hair—but none of them limped. "I'll be there as soon as I can."

Everybody looked up as Nick entered the dining room. "Sorry I'm late," he said as he took his seat between Sean, Al's thirteen-year-old grandson, and Sean's seven-year-old sister, Alicia. Al shot him a dirty look from his seat at the head of the table. A roast ham sat on a platter in front of him.

"Give Nick some ham, Al," Helen said. The grandfather clock in the corner chimed seven times. Seven o'clock. Nick passed his plate to Al but he didn't have much of an appetite. While everybody here was enjoying a roast ham with all the trimmings, his dad was back in his cell, locked in for the night.

"How did the game go?" asked Leo, Sean and Alicia's father.

"We beat Langley 8–1."

"Langley sucks," said Sean dismissively.

"Watch your language, Sean," his mother told him.

"Wait till you play Hollyburn," Sean whispered to Nick. "They're gonna kick your ass."

The little shit is probably right, Nick thought. It was going to take a team effort to beat Hollyburn and the Lightning were nowhere close to being a team.

Helen bowed her head. Everybody else did likewise. Sunday dinner always began with the same prayer. "God grant us the serenity to accept the things we cannot change, the courage to change the things we can, and the wisdom to know the difference."

Nick heard the words, but he wasn't paying attention to them. All he could think about was his father sitting in his cell, filling out his application to be transferred to another prison.

CHAPTER FIFTEEN

Nick stepped off the bus in front of the school. Ivan was on the sidewalk, talking to a couple of friends. He saw Nick and came over to him.

"You missed a great game yesterday," he said.

"So I heard." Seattle had creamed the Raiders, 27-7.

"I like the Seahawks' chances to make the playoffs."

"Me too."

Sherry was down the street, coming in their direction. Nick's heart skipped a beat. "Do you know if Jennifer's seen Sherry with that college guy again?" he asked.

"She hasn't said anything. Why?"

"Just curious," Nick said.

Ivan glanced at Sherry. "Just curious, huh?" he said with a grin.

Sherry walked up to them. "Hey, guys."

"I'll catch you later," Ivan said. He winked at Nick and walked away.

"I hear you won yesterday," Sherry said.

"Don't tell me you've become a fan?"

Sherry shook her head. "Amy told me." Amy was Sherry's nine-year-old sister and Nick's biggest fan. "She said you played really well."

"I'm getting there, but I still have a long way to go."

"When's your next game?" she asked.

"Wednesday. Against Surrey." *My turn to ask a question,*

Nick thought, but there was only one question on his mind and it was the one question he couldn't ask: *Are you still seeing Joe College?* "Have you decided where you're going next year?"

"I want to go to the Ontario College of Art and Design in Toronto, but Mom wants me to stay here and go to Emily Carr or UBC."

"Going to school in Toronto would be cool," he said as they walked through the front door. *If she's thinking of going away,* he thought, *she's either not going out with Joe College anymore, or she isn't serious about him.* But his heart sank at the thought of Sherry being on the other side of the country.

"There's no guarantee I'll get in," she said.

"Are you kidding? Once they see your paintings, you'll get in for sure."

Sherry shrugged. "See you later," she said.

"Later." Nick watched Sherry head for her class and thought back to the first time he saw her paintings. He wondered if she was thinking of it as well.

It was the day they had sex for the first time. Sherry was the one who initiated it, which had taken Nick by surprise. They'd done a lot of stuff by then, but whenever he said he wanted to have sex, she said she wasn't ready.

It was during the trial. His dad had dropped him off at Sherry's house. He hadn't said a word to Nick on the drive over. Nick knew he was worried about the verdict. For the first time Nick let himself consider the possibility that his father would be found guilty.

Sherry walked up beside him as his dad drove off. She took his hand in hers without saying a word. An electric charge surged through his body, as if they had somehow become one person. He felt she knew exactly what he was thinking and feeling. They stood there silently until his dad turned the corner and disappeared. "Come," she said, and led him upstairs to her bedroom.

It was the second time in his life Nick had slept with a girl. The first was the summer before he met Sherry. Nick got drunk at a beach party and ended up in bed with a girl from Prince Rupert. The next day he woke up feeling as if he'd crossed a bridge that divided the world in two, between people who'd had sex and people who hadn't, but after the initial excitement wore off, it didn't seem like such a big deal. Not that he wanted to go back or anything. It was more a case of "Okay, I did that. Now what?"

What he and Sherry did felt completely different from what he did with the girl from Prince Rupert. That had just been physical. With Sherry it was emotional too. And it didn't end when they were finished. Afterwards he and Sherry held onto each other for a long time.

"That was nice," she said.

"It was," he answered. He couldn't think of anything else to say. Then they did it a second time. Later, Sherry showed him a series of self-portraits she had painted when she was at her grandmother's place. Two of the pictures were nudes. She hadn't shown them to anybody else. Nick knew she was showing him for the same reason she had slept with him: because she trusted him and because she loved him.

Two weeks later Nick's father was convicted, and shortly after that, Nick stopped returning Sherry's calls.

CHAPTER SIXTEEN

"I'll meet you out front after the game," Nick said to Google. They were in the hallway of the Pacific Coliseum. There were eight minutes left in the game, but with the Giants down 4–0, the disgruntled fans were already heading for the exit. Google nodded and walked away.

Nick and Google were looking for the bald guy with no eyebrows they had seen at the Giants game the previous week. Nick didn't hold out much hope. They hadn't seen him in the crowd during the game, or in the corridors during either intermission, so chances were he wasn't there.

Nick moved slowly toward the exit. He'd hurt his ankle the night before in the game against Surrey, a game the Lightning lost 4–1. It was just a slight sprain, not bad enough to keep him out of today's practice. The loss was more painful. Surrey had manhandled the Lightning, confirming that the easy wins over Chilliwack and Langley were no indication that the team was getting its act together.

Just then Kenny Lipton appeared with his dad, a big hulking man who came to all the games, mainly, it seemed, to yell at his son and criticize the referees.

"Hey, Kenny."

"Hey."

"Who's your friend?" Lipton's father asked.

"This is Nick Macklin. He's on the team."

"Of course. Didn't recognize you out of uniform," Mr. Lipton said. An awkward silence followed as he realized who Nick was; more accurately, when he realized who Nick's father was. Nick was used to it. People never knew what to say to him once they made the connection.

"That was a stinker," Lipton's dad said finally, pointing his thumb back toward the rink. "A total waste of time."

A total waste of time, Nick repeated to himself. *That's how he describes a night out with his son?*

"At least I didn't pay for the tickets. Earl Taylor gave me a couple of comps. He and I go way back," he said proudly, as if he expected Nick to be impressed that he was a friend of the Giants' assistant coach.

"They're pretty bad," Nick said. He didn't know what else to say.

"Almost as bad as you guys." Lipton's father chuckled at his own wit. "Good to see you back out there. Kenny can use some help. He can't carry the team by himself."

Kenny stared at his shoes. Nick almost felt sorry for him. Mr. Lipton carried on, oblivious to his son's discomfort. "The scout from Michigan was real interested in Kenny last year. Said he had a good chance for a scholarship. I've been calling him to tell him how good Kenny's playing this year, but he hasn't come out to watch 'cause the team's so bad."

"That's not the reason he hasn't come," Kenny said.

His dad stared him down. "I don't remember you being in on the conversation, sport." Kenny lowered his head. "That's right. Don't speak when you don't know what you're talking about. All right, let's get going." He turned to Nick. "See you tomorrow. You guys better step it up, or Richmond's going to bury you just like Surrey did."

Not what you'd call words of encouragement, Nick thought, as

Lipton and his dad walked away. But he was right. The team was going to have to get its act together if they were going to give Richmond a game.

McAndrew had summed it up after today's practice. "You guys are like two mules pulling in opposite directions. Until you're all headed the same way, the wagon isn't going anywhere." Lipton had scored the Lightning's lone goal against Surrey but had, once again, shown that he had as much interest in playing defense as he had in contracting leprosy. The way Nick and his friends saw it, there was only one mule that needed to turn around.

"Two households, both alike in dignity, in fair Verona where we lay our scene." Nick had been staring at the opening lines of *Romeo and Juliet* for the past five minutes. He closed the book. There was no point trying to get into it now. He was too tense to concentrate.

Nick and Google hadn't seen the guy with no eyebrows after the game, but that wasn't the source of his anxiety. Nor was tomorrow night's match against Richmond, although there was good reason to be concerned on that front as well.

Nick was thinking about his visit to the prison on Saturday. For the first time ever, he wasn't looking forward to seeing his father. In fact he was dreading it. He and his dad had always been a team, working toward the same goal. Now it felt like they were on different sides.

Nick went downstairs to get a snack. As he passed Al's office, Al motioned for him to come in.

"The estate sale is on Monday," Al said, "so if you want anything else from the house, you'll have to get over there before then."

Nick shook his head. "I've got everything I want," he

said. He had gone to the house earlier in the week, after his dad called to say their home had been purchased and that the contents were being sold off, and he had absolutely no desire to go back. It had been one of the most depressing days of his life. Every single item, down to the pots and pans, had a price sticker on it in preparation for the sale. All his memories had been reduced to dollars and cents. There was a sign inside the front door—by now it would be stuck in the lawn—that said ESTATE SALE. Nick had looked the term up on Wikipedia when he got back to the house. "An estate sale is a type of garage sale. The most common reason for an estate sale is the death of the property owner."

The death of the property owner. No, he wouldn't be going back to the house any time soon.

Nick headed to the door. "One more thing," Al said. "The library on Georgia, the one you said you were at when I called you on Sunday? It closes at five on Sundays."

"I was …"

Al held up his hand. "I don't want to know. If your father asks me what you've been up to, I don't want to have to tell him something he should be hearing from you. And I especially don't want to tell him you've been lying to me. Fair enough?" Nick nodded. "A word of advice, Nick. Next time you invent a story, come up with something that's not so easy to check out."

Like telling everybody you've stopped betting, Nick felt like saying. He wondered if he should tell his dad about Al's gambling. Then again, maybe he shouldn't. He'd have to explain what he was doing at a Giants game, and he definitely didn't want to do that. Besides, there wasn't anything his dad could do about it. Not from inside a prison cell.

CHAPTER SEVENTEEN

Nick had tossed and turned all night, and his stomach was still churning when they passed the exit to Langley. They'd be at the prison in less than an hour. He told himself everything would be fine, but he didn't really believe it.

Helen was singing along to a song on the car radio. Nick glanced at her. For a moment, silhouetted against the sun, she looked like a young girl. Helen had been a presence in his life ever since Nick could remember, but he'd never really gotten to know her until he moved in with the Hawkins. Al had always been at the house or at his dad's games, but he saw much less of Helen. She was friendly enough, but he never had much to do with her. In the past year he'd come to like her a lot, even if he didn't show it very often. He respected her too. It couldn't be easy for her to have a surly teenager in the house, but she'd been great: understanding enough to cut him some slack, and tough enough to call him out whenever he crossed the line.

"Do you know this song?" Helen asked when the music came to an end. Nick shook his head. "*Tupelo Honey,* by Van Morrison," she said. "Every time I hear it, it takes me back to my high school prom. Al and I had been going out for a couple of months, but we broke up a week before the dance. I can't remember why. I didn't feel like going, but there was no way I was staying at home, either. I got a friend of my sister's to take me: Mike Casey, a big, good-looking guy. He was in third-year university. I wanted to make Al jealous." Helen smiled at the memory. "Al came with a girl from another school. She was very pretty. I guess he was trying to make me jealous too. We ignored each other all night, but somehow we were both alone when this song came on. Al came over and asked me to dance. We've been together ever since."

She really loves the guy, Nick thought. If she finds out he's started gambling again, she's going to be heartbroken.

"Did you get the real estate documents?" Helen asked, after Nick's dad sat down at the table in the visiting room.

"I mailed them back yesterday," he said.

"It's a good time to sell," Helen said. "Interest rates won't stay this low for long."

Nick's dad nodded. "Everybody says the market is headed for a fall," he said.

Who gives a shit? Nick said to himself. *The market can fall into the frigging ocean for all I care.* He got to his feet. "I'm going to get a pop," he said. "Anybody want one?"

"No thanks," they said at the same time.

"How did it go against Richmond?" his dad asked when they were in the bullpen.

"We won, 4–3."

Nick's dad waited for him to elaborate, but Nick didn't feel like supplying any more details. In the past he would have told his father all about the game. He would have told him how Ivan broke out of his slump with a bang, scoring the winning goal with less than two minutes left in the game. He would have described how his friend split the Richmond defense, kicking the puck ahead with his feet before firing a bullet into the top right corner of the net. He would have told his dad how Kenny Lipton sulked like a little baby after the game because he'd been held off the score sheet. He would have complained about Lipton's lack of effort on the defensive end, and wondered why McAndrew continued to let him get away with it. He would have told his father everything, but he was so angry with him that he didn't feel like saying anything.

"How did you play?"

"Pretty good." The truth was that he played great. It wasn't just that he scored one goal and assisted on another, it was the way he controlled the game when he was on the ice. Even McAndrew was impressed. "Keep this up and I'll be forced to give you some more ice time," the coach told him after the game. Nick knew how pleased his dad would be to hear that, but he kept it to himself.

"What's wrong, Nick?" his father asked.

"Nothing. Just tired, I guess." His father gave him a disbelieving look. Nick could see the disappointment in his eyes. He felt like a real shit, but he couldn't help himself.

"Your dad's doing well," Helen said, as she and Nick walked out of the prison.

"Whatever," Nick said.

Helen looked at him. "Are you okay?"

"I'm fine." He usually felt sad after a visit, knowing it would be a few weeks before he'd see his father again. He was sad now for a different reason. The visit had been a disaster, but that wasn't what he was thinking about. It was what happened afterwards that bothered him. As he and Helen were leaving the visiting room, he saw his father talking to Leon. His dad was laughing at something Leon had said. Leon. Frigging Leon. The guy his dad had told him to stay away from because he was a real prick! Just thinking about it made Nick furious. Take away the uniform, and you would have thought you were looking at two buddies shooting the shit. His dad seemed to be right at home.

Nick got in the car, turned on the engine, and gunned it out of the parking lot. He couldn't get out of there fast enough.

CHAPTER EIGHTEEN

"Is that new?" Nick asked. He pointed at a painting of a young woman on the wall over Dr. Davis's desk. She was lying on her back in a field, staring up at the clouds.

"I got it a few months ago," Davis answered. Nick nodded. The painting was the only thing that had changed in the six months since Nick told Davis that therapy was "a waste of freaking time" and stormed out of his office.

Davis sat in his chair, his long legs stretched out in front of him and crossed at the ankles. Nick didn't know if Davis could help him, but he didn't have anywhere else to turn. He was so upset by the visit with his dad that he'd barely slept for the past two nights. He had texted Davis from math class that morning. I need to see you. Davis got back to him right away. I can see you at 5 p.m.

"How are you, Nick?" Davis asked.

"Okay."

Davis sat there waiting for Nick to say something. Now that he was here, Nick didn't feel like talking. His eyes wandered to the painting. He wished he could trade places with the young woman. She looked so peaceful. *What's the point of talking about any of this? It isn't going to change anything.* He looked back at Davis who waited patiently for him to speak.

"I went to see my father on Saturday," he said. Davis gave him an encouraging nod. *I don't want to get into it, I really don't.* A few seconds passed.

"And how was that?" Davis asked.

"How do you think?" Nick said aggressively.

"I don't know. Why don't you tell me?"

"It was terrible, okay?" Nick could hear the anguish in his voice. The image of his dad joking around with Leon burned in his mind.

"What was so terrible about it?" Davis said.

Nick didn't answer. Davis gave him another encouraging nod. *What the hell,* he thought. *I'm here, I might as well say something.* "My dad's given up," he said in a lifeless tone of voice. "He's given up." Then he told Davis everything that had happened, how his father had accepted the fact that he was going to be in jail for a long, long time, and that he'd said Nick should accept it too. "Screw that," Nick said angrily. "He can give up, but I'm not going to."

He told Davis that he was going to keep looking for Baldy, no matter what his dad said. Nick didn't have to worry about Davis spilling the beans. Everything a patient tells a psychiatrist is confidential. It was one of the rules. It was a good one, Nick thought. It meant he could feel free to say whatever was on his mind.

There was a lot on his mind, and it all came rushing out: all the anger he felt toward his father. Nick was angry with him for putting the house up for sale, for reading his stupid books on meditation, and for a million other things. But it all boiled down to Nick being angry with him for giving up, and for expecting Nick to give up too. He didn't know how long he talked, but he talked until he was all talked out. You were supposed to feel better when you got things off your chest, but he didn't feel better. He felt worse. He felt like his father had betrayed him. And he felt like he had betrayed his father.

"I know it doesn't make any sense. I know he has to accept that he's in jail, or he'll go crazy," Nick continued, "but that doesn't change the way I feel." He held up his hand to stop Davis from speaking. "I know. I'm entitled to my feelings, right?" That was another rule. When it came to how you felt, there was no right or wrong when you were in therapy. It didn't matter that he was a selfish prick for being angry with his dad. It only mattered that he *was* angry.

"That's what it says in the manual," Davis said with a smile. "Why do you think you're so angry?"

"I just told you," Nick said angrily. "Because he's given up."

"What do you want him to do?"

"I don't know. Something. Anything. I don't know who he is anymore. He never used to take crap from anybody."

"It sounds like you feel that the man you visited on Saturday and the man you've known all your life are two different people."

"Exactly. It's like an alien has taken over his body."

"The father you grew up with is the hockey star, the man everybody looked up to and respected, the man the other guys all wished was their father. Not the man in a prison who has no power, who has to do whatever he's told, the man your friends feel sorry for. You feel that you've lost your father." Nick could feel tears welling up in his eyes. That was it. He felt as if he'd lost his father. He took a Kleenex out of the box on the table and blew his nose.

"Every boy wants a strong father figure," Davis continued, "a role model who can show him what it means to be a man. Your dad was a great role model, not because he was a hockey star, but because he was responsible and

87

loving and courageous and loyal and honest and because he treated everybody with respect. His circumstances may have changed, Nick, but his character hasn't. He's still all of those things. He's the same man you've known all your life."

Maybe so, Nick thought, but he still couldn't get the picture of his father and Leon out of his head. He noticed Davis looking at his watch.

"That's all the time we have for today," Nick said in a sarcastic voice, mimicking what Davis always said at the end of a session.

Davis laughed. "Do you want to schedule another appointment?" Nick shrugged. Davis consulted his agenda. "I can see you next Monday at the same time."

"Whatever."

"Is that a yes or a no?"

Nick shrugged again. He didn't know if he wanted to see Davis again or not. He wasn't as angry as he was when the session started. But he was a lot sadder.

"Why don't you think about it and let me know?" Davis said after a few seconds.

"Next Monday's good," Nick said. Then he opened the door and walked out of the room.

CHAPTER NINETEEN

"Let's do it, bud," Nick said to Ivan as they stepped onto the ice Wednesday night for the warm-up before the game against the Aldergrove Bears.

Red caught up to them as they circled the net. "Gonna kick some ass tonight!" he screamed.

Two days earlier Nick had his best game of the season in a 1–1 tie against the Burnaby Owls. And at yesterday's practice McAndrew had reunited him with Red and Ivan, hoping they would kick-start the team's sluggish offense. The three of them had clicked right off the bat. It was as if Nick had never been away. After so many years of playing together, they knew where they were each going to be before they got there. The move energized the entire team. It was their best practice all season. Even McAndrew was pleased. "That's a start," he said, when he came into the locker room after practice. "Now let's see if you can keep it up for the rest of the year."

"The Three Amigos are back!" Red crowed, after McAndrew left.

"The Three Stooges is more like it," Lipton muttered to Josh Parry as Nick walked past his chair. Nick ignored the comment. He'd do his talking on the ice.

"Nick, Ivan, Red. You're on," McAndrew bellowed two minutes into the game. The three of them hopped over the

89

boards as the Aldergrove center carried the puck out from behind his net. Nick met him at the blue line, forcing him to dump the puck off to one of his wingers, who slapped it into the Lightning's zone. Biggie corralled the puck and whipped it across the ice to Ivan. He carried it over center and fired it around the boards, into the far corner. Nick headed for the net as Red raced down the right wing. Red and the Aldergrove defenseman reached the puck at the same time. Red bounced his opponent off the puck long enough to slap it along the boards to Nick. He faked in one direction and then came out in front of the net, drawing the other Aldergrove defenseman over to him before sliding the puck across the crease to Ivan, who banged it home.

"All right!" Nick yelled. He skated over to Ivan to congratulate him.

"Yes!" Red roared, as he jumped onto the two of them, sending all three to the ice.

Ivan scored twice more before the first period ended, and Red added another in the third period, whipping a wrist shot into the upper corner after taking a beautiful drop pass from Nick. Between them, the line scored four goals in a 7–3 trouncing of the second place Bears. It was the team's best game by far and its biggest win of the season. The exuberant post-game celebration in the locker room made it clear that the team felt it had finally turned the corner.

Everybody milled around the room, congratulating each other on the victory: everybody except Kenny Lipton. He was slumped on a chair across from Nick, a sour look on his face, as he contemplated his second scoreless game in a row.

"Somebody got the monkey off his back," Nick said as Ivan sat down beside him.

"With a little help from his friends," Ivan replied.

"And don't you forget it," Red said. "You're nothing without Nick and me."

"Luckiest hat trick I ever saw," Lipton grumbled to Josh Parry. "The Aldergrove goalie should have had a white cane instead of a stick."

Nick looked at Ivan. He shrugged. No point getting involved. But Red couldn't let it go. "Nice plus minus tonight, Kenny," he said sarcastically. All three of the Aldergrove goals had been scored when Lipton was on the ice, mainly because he seemed to be allergic to entering the Lightning's defensive zone.

"Piss off," Lipton said, as McAndrew came into the room. The first words out of his mouth put an end to the celebration.

"If you guys think a half-assed effort like that is going to do the job against Hollyburn, you've got another think coming. You want to win the championship? Then every single player has to give one hundred per cent on every single shift. On both ends of the ice." Nick looked over at Lipton. He was staring at his skates. McAndrew didn't mention any names. He didn't have to.

"He's playing favorites," Red complained at Mike's, the diner across the street from the arena where they always went after a game. He was pissed that McAndrew hadn't singled Lipton out for his lack of hustle. "Look how he yelled at Biggie for getting a penalty at the end of the first period."

Biggie looked up from his submarine sandwich. "It was a dumb penalty," he said, as he polished off the rest of the sub. He called to the cook behind the counter. "Gimme another one, Mike."

"That's not the point," Red said. "He should treat everyone the same. If he's going to yell at Biggie in front of everybody, he should do the same with Lipton."

Nick didn't agree that McAndrew should treat everyone the same. His dad always said that 90 per cent of coaching is knowing how to deal with your players. "Lots of coaches know their Xs and Os," he'd say, "but a good coach has to understand people." McAndrew had jumped all over Biggie in the locker room because he knew Biggie could handle it. "Stupid penalty. Stupid, stupid penalty," he had said, getting right into Biggie's face. "What was going through your thick skull?" Biggie had just nodded. He knew there was no excuse for getting a penalty at center ice with ten seconds left in the period, and he wouldn't do it again. He didn't take the criticism personally.

"I don't know how you do it, Big," Google said. "Doesn't it make you mad?"

Biggie shook his head. "You gotta ignore the anger and hear the message."

Easier said than done, Nick thought. He hated it when a coach yelled at him in front of his teammates. He responded better when his mistakes were pointed out in private. That was probably the case with Lipton too. McAndrew was giving him a chance to get his act together. The coach wanted to win, and if Lipton played the way he was capable of playing, McAndrew knew the team had a better chance of winning. But in the end, if all Kenny Lipton cared about was Kenny Lipton, the team was better off without him.

CHAPTER TWENTY

With exams less than three weeks away, Nick knew he should be concentrating on his biology homework, but he was fighting a losing battle. He and Google had taken advantage of the team's day off following the win against Aldergrove to go to a Junior B game in North Vancouver to look for Baldy. It was the fourth game at four different arenas that they'd gone to in the past week, but the outing was as unsuccessful as the other three.

A single unwelcome thought kept running through Nick's head as he sat at his desk. It had grabbed him while he was on the bus on the way back to the house, and it hadn't let go. His father was right. It *would* take a miracle to find Baldy. There had to be another way to prove his dad was innocent.

But how? Nick had gone down this road countless times before. He always ended up asking the same question: Who else might have wanted to kill Marty Albertson? The private detectives hired by Nick's father had dug into every aspect of Albertson's life, trying to find someone with a motive—someone other than his dad. They had come up empty.

Nick had gone over the case so many times that by now, he knew Albertson's bio by heart. By the time he was fourteen Albertson was receiving more national attention than any player since Wayne Gretzky. At sixteen he was the star player for the Kingston Frontenacs. Then, one night, he and a couple of teammates got drunk, stole a car, and went for a joyride. Albertson was driving, and he lost control on a patch of ice. The car slammed into a ditch and rolled over. Both his teammates were injured, but Albertson walked away without a scratch. He moved to BC to get a fresh start and joined the Kelowna Rockets, where he became the top junior in the country.

Even though Nick was only nine at the time, he remembered how excited everyone was when the Canucks won the draft lottery and chose Albertson as their number one pick. He was supposed to lead the team to the promised land—the Stanley Cup—but he never lived up to his potential. He was more interested in chasing women than chasing the puck. "He's the only player I know who leads the league in scoring without putting on his skates," Nick's father used to say. Three years ago the team had finally given up on Albertson and traded him to the Leafs.

After the hit, Albertson left the country to escape from all the bad press. He spent the summer travelling in Asia. The detective agency sent a man to retrace his journey on the hunch that something had happened along the way that might have led to his murder.

Nick had a copy of the detective's report in his desk. He took it out and read through it again, hoping he'd see something he'd missed before.

There had been one promising lead. Albertson had an affair with a married woman in Hong Kong. The woman's husband, an Australian millionaire with ties to organized crime, found out about it and threatened to kill him. Albertson must have taken the threat seriously because he left Hong Kong the next day.

Nick remembered how excited they were when the

detective emailed the information. It was the first good news they'd had since his dad's arrest. Finally they had another suspect. But twenty-four hours later, another email brought them back down to earth. The day after Albertson left Hong Kong, the millionaire and his wife, along with the entire crew, drowned when their yacht was caught in a typhoon and sank on the way back to Australia.

Nick leafed through the report. After Albertson left Hong Kong, he spent the last week of his vacation at a resort in the Philippines. Nothing much happened there. He spent his days lounging by the pool and his nights gambling at the casino, accompanied by a young actress from New Zealand. She was single. Albertson had apparently learned his lesson in Hong Kong. On September 16, he returned to Vancouver. Two days later he was murdered.

Nick tossed the report onto his desk. He was back at square one. Despite all the time and effort that had been put into investigating Albertson's life, they hadn't found anybody with a motive to kill him. Anybody except Nick's father.

CHAPTER TWENTY-ONE

Nick and his dad sat at a table in the corner of the visiting room. Nick wondered why there was no one else in the room.

"I read your assignment, and you know what I think?" Nick's dad said. "I think Dylan Thomas is full of shit." Nick was confused. He didn't remember showing the assignment to his father.

His dad picked a pack of cigarettes up off the table. "Want one?" Nick shook his head. *When did Dad start smoking? And why would he offer me one?*

"Mr. Putnam says Dylan Thomas is one of the greatest writers of the twentieth century."

"I never heard of Putnam. Who does he play for?" His dad laughed so hard that tears ran down his cheeks.

"He's my English teacher," Nick said. He thought he'd mentioned Putnam to his dad before, but maybe he hadn't. He looked up as Pete came into the room. He was limping—Nick had never noticed the limp before—and he was wearing a baseball cap. That's not part of a guard's uniform, Nick thought.

"Visiting hours are over," Pete said. He took off his cap and scratched his head. It was as bald as a baby's butt. Nick's dad tucked the pack of cigarettes under the sleeve of his T-shirt.

"Listen, Nick, I appreciate everything you're doing but

don't bother bringing me any more poems. I shot Marty Albertson, and if I had to do it over, I'd shoot him again. That prick deserved to die. You should've seen the look in his eyes before I pulled the trigger. It was beautiful. Worth every second I'll have to spend in this place. I know it's tough on you, kid, but you'll get over it." He gave Nick a fist jab. "Peace in the Middle East," he said. Then he stood up, pointed his hand at his own head as if it was a gun, and pretended to pull the trigger.

"A bald guy with a limp," Pete said to his dad, shaking his head. "Did you actually think anybody would buy that?"

"Hey, it was the best I could come up with," his dad said with a shrug. He looked at Nick solemnly, and then burst out laughing. Nick started laughing too, laughing until his cheeks hurt. "See you in a couple of weeks, sport," his dad said when he stopped laughing. He went to the door that led back to the cells and rang the buzzer. It rang and rang.

Nick awoke up with a start. It took a few seconds to realize that the ringing sound was coming from the alarm on his bedside table. He reached over and turned it off, then lay there trying to make sense of his dream.

Dr. Davis said that dreams reveal the dreamer's hidden thoughts and desires. So why did he dream that his dad confessed to killing Albertson? Was it because, deep down, he thought his father was guilty? What was it Pete said in his dream? "A bald guy with a limp. Did you actually think anybody would buy that?"

Nick remembered how the Crown Attorney had summed up the case in his final speech to the jury. "Mr. Macklin told the police he had never been in Mr. Albertson's condominium. So when the police found paint on his suit jacket that matched the paint in the condominium he had to come up with a story, and he had to come up with it quickly. That's when he invented the bald man with the limp. Where is this bald man with a limp?" the Crown Attorney asked, pasting a pretend puzzled look on his face. "Everybody has been looking for him. But nobody has found him. The explanation is simple. The only place he exists is in Steve Macklin's imagination."

That wasn't the only problem with his dad's story. He told the police that Albertson was supposed to come to their house in West Van, but according to Albertson's BlackBerry, the meeting was to take place at his condo in Point Grey. Nick's father said it couldn't have been a misunderstanding. He said that Albertson had asked for directions to the house. Nick's dad said that the real killer must have changed the entry in Albertson's BlackBerry as part of his plan to frame him. The Crown Attorney said there was a simpler explanation. He said Nick's dad was lying. "When Mr. Macklin told the police the meeting was at his house, he didn't know they had already found Mr. Albertson's BlackBerry. By the time he found out, it was too late to change his story."

Nick stared at the ceiling. He didn't care what the Crown Attorney said. The bald man was out there. They just hadn't found him yet. No, his dream didn't mean that he thought his father was guilty. He knew his dad didn't kill Albertson: knew it from the bottom of his heart. But there was something else about the dream that troubled him, something he couldn't put his finger on.

He reached for his phone and scrolled through his contacts until he got to Dr. Davis.

CHAPTER TWENTY-TWO

"Interesting," Davis said after Nick recounted his dream.

Nick was in biology class when Davis texted him back to say he had an opening at three o'clock. Luckily, Nick had a spare last period, but he would have skipped class to make it. He hadn't stopped thinking about the dream all day. He knew it would plague him all weekend if he had to wait until Monday for an appointment.

Interesting? What the hell does that mean? Nick wondered.

"How did you feel when your dad confessed?" Davis asked.

Nick forced himself back into his dream. "I was happy," he said after thinking about it for a while. He felt confused. That's what had been bothering him. His dad had just admitted he'd murdered Albertson, and he was happy. It made no sense. "Why would I be happy?" he asked.

"What do you think?" Davis answered.

"You're the expert. You tell me."

"What do you mean by happy?" Davis asked.

"I don't know. It wasn't like I was jumping for joy, it was more like a weight had been lifted off my shoulders."

"You felt relieved," Davis suggested.

"Yeah. Relieved."

"Why would you be relieved?" From the way he asked, Nick was pretty sure Davis knew the answer to his question.

"You tell me," he repeated.

"You said you felt like a weight had been lifted off your shoulders. What do you mean by a weight?"

Enough with the questions already. "I don't know. It's just a saying."

"Maybe. But in a way you have been carrying a weight since your father went to jail, haven't you?"

"What do you mean? What weight have I been carrying?"

"Not a weight exactly. More like a burden. The burden of getting your dad out of jail."

"That's not a burden. He's my father."

"You've been looking for Baldy for a long time," Davis said sympathetically.

"Ever since Dad was convicted."

"It must be frustrating not to have found him."

"You think?" Nick said angrily. Davis had no idea how frustrated he was. He'd been looking for Baldy for a year. One entire year of riding buses and hanging out in hockey arenas, looking for a needle in a haystack with no guarantee that the needle was even *in* the goddamn haystack. He felt frustrated, all right. And Angry. And … hopeless.

"But you have to keep trying, don't you? What kind of son would sit around and do nothing while his father is in prison?" *Exactly,* Nick thought. *I couldn't live with myself.* "But if your dad was guilty, you could stop looking for Baldy. You'd be off the hook."

"What are you saying? That I don't want to keep looking for Baldy?"

Davis waited a few moments before answering. "Do you?" he asked, a serious expression on his face.

"Or course I do!" Nick shouted. "I have to find him or

Dad will never get out of jail." He glared at Davis, then turned away and looked at the girl in the painting. A wave of sadness swept over him. He couldn't deny it anymore. He could ride a bus and hang out in hockey arenas for the rest of his life, but he was never going to find Baldy. Tears welled up in his eyes. He looked back at Davis. "I have to keep looking. I have to," he said.

"You've put yourself in an impossible situation," Davis said gently. "Your brain is telling you that there's nothing you can do to get your dad out of jail. But your heart is telling you that if you stop trying, you're a bad son ... You're not a bad son, Nick. You're a wonderful son and your father knows that."

Nick stared at Davis, an agonized look on his face. Then he burst into tears, crying like he had never cried before. Not even when his mom died. "I did my best. I did my best."

CHAPTER TWENTY-THREE

"Thanks for calling," Nick said.

"No problem," Dr. Davis said. "See you tomorrow."

Nick put his cellphone back in his pocket, and walked toward the front door of Mike's Diner, towing his hockey bag behind him.

It had been two days since his session, and Davis had called to see how he was doing. Nick had told him he was okay, and that was the truth. It had been a tough couple of days. It hadn't been easy to decide to stop looking for Baldy. He couldn't help feeling like he was abandoning his father, but whenever he second-guessed the decision, he ran headfirst into a brick wall. There was no getting around the reality that finding Baldy was a hopeless task. Once he accepted that fact there was no going back, and even though that saddened him, he knew he'd be able to deal with it.

Ivan, Biggie, and Red were already seated at a booth in the diner. Nick slid into the seat beside Ivan. "It's official," Nick said. "Your slump is over."

Ivan had scored two goals in a 5–1 victory over a good Ridge Meadows team, giving him seven goals in the past four games.

"A blind man could have scored with the way you set me up," Ivan said. He was being too modest, as usual. Nick had assisted on both of Ivan's goals, with passes that gave him clear shots at the net, but not many players could have threaded the needle the way Ivan had.

"We keep playing like this, we'll go all the way," Red said.

"Let's see how good we are when we play Hollyburn on Thursday," Biggie cautioned.

"We'll beat 'em," Red said confidently. "They only beat Ridge Meadows by a goal last week. At Hollyburn."

They were still discussing their chances a few minutes later when Google came through the door and joined them at the booth. "Well?" Red asked.

"Well what?" Google asked, feigning ignorance. He knew exactly what Red was referring to. They all did.

"What did McAndrew say to Lipton?" Red asked impatiently. Lipton had put in another lackluster performance, turning it on only when he had a chance to score. McAndrew had summoned him to his office after the game.

"How should I know?" Google asked. "I wasn't in on the meeting. I was too busy picking up your smelly uniforms."

"You must have heard something," Red said.

"McAndrew does have a loud voice," Google admitted with a grin. "He was very calm. Told Lipton that he had the talent to be the best player in the league, but it wouldn't mean anything unless he put out the effort."

"Best player in the league," Red snorted. "Everybody knows Ivan's the best."

"I'm not even close," Ivan said. *Another typical Ivan reaction,* Nick thought, but he agreed with him. Lipton was the most talented guy he'd ever played with. "You saw the goal he scored tonight," Ivan pointed out, referring to the bullet Lipton fired from just inside the blue line that the

Ridge Meadow goalie could only wave at.

"I don't care how good he is. McAndrew should kick his lazy ass off the team."

"That's not going to happen, Red." Biggie turned to Nick. "Are you going to eat the rest of those fries?"

"Don't you ever think of anything except your stomach?" Red asked, as Nick passed his plate to Biggie.

"You want to win the championship?" Ivan asked. "Our chances are a helluva lot better if Lipton plays the way he's capable of playing. McAndrew's no fool." Nick nodded. No coach in his right mind would want to lose a scorer like Lipton unless it was absolutely necessary.

Biggie's cellphone rang. He flipped it open. "Hey, babe." It was Biggie's girlfriend. He stood up and walked away from the table.

"I was wrong," Red whispered so Biggie couldn't hear. "He thinks about more than his stomach. Big man's going to get waxed tonight." He looked at the others, hoping for a laugh. He didn't get one.

Nick watched Biggie talking on the phone, then looked at his other friends around the table. They were still boys, but Biggie was a man. It had nothing to do with his size. It had to do with the fact that he knew who he was. He didn't waste his time trying to impress anyone. Nick remembered his dad telling him how important it was to find your own path in life. "What other people think of you is none of your business," was the way he put it. It had taken Nick a while to figure that one out.

Biggie came over to the table. "I'm going to see Heather. See you guys later." A perfect example, Nick thought. Most guys would be too embarrassed to admit they were leaving their buddies to go see a girlfriend. Not Biggie. He didn't give it a second thought.

"Seahawks win today, and they're guaranteed a wild card spot," Red said as he, Nick, and Google piled into Ivan's car.

"Pittsburgh's tough," Google said skeptically. "They've got the best defense in the league."

"Seattle will tear them apart," Red said.

Nick settled back in his seat and let his mind wander as his friends talked about the football game. None of them had made a big deal when he said he was coming to Ivan's to watch it even though it was the first time he'd joined them all year. But it felt like a big deal to Nick. It was like putting an exclamation point on his decision to stop looking for Baldy. He exchanged a quick look with Google. Nick had let him know the day before about his decision. Saying the words out loud had been harder than he expected. He felt like he was admitting that his father was never going to leave prison.

He felt a twinge of guilt as Ivan pulled out of the parking lot, but it didn't last. Truth was, he was glad he wasn't roaming around the city looking for a ghost. He glanced at Google. He was pretty sure Google was glad too.

CHAPTER TWENTY-FOUR

"Romeo's a tool," said Fred Feldman. The class erupted in laughter. Nick noticed that Sherry was laughing too. Fred stood at his desk, grinning from ear to ear.

"Would you care to expand on that insight, Mr. Feldman?" asked Putnam, with mock solemnity. "Why is Romeo a 'tool', as you so eloquently put it?" Everybody laughed again.

"For killing himself," Freddie said, as if it was obvious. "I know he thinks his chick's dead, but offing himself isn't going to bring her back to life."

"He kills himself because he can't bear to live without Juliet," Emma Jenkins said. "That's the whole point of the play. Shakespeare is saying that love is the most powerful thing in the world. It's even more powerful than death." She looked at Putnam, eager to score some brownie points. "Juliet kills herself for the same reason."

"Juliet's a tool too," Freddie said, right on cue. Even Putnam couldn't help laughing. Nick wouldn't have put it the way Freddie did, but he basically agreed. He liked the play right up to the last scene, but he hated the ending. It wasn't romantic, it was just plain stupid. If Romeo had waited ten minutes, Juliet would have woken up and the two of them would have lived happily ever after. Just like it happened in the stories his parents read to him when he was little.

He couldn't remember when things changed, when stories stopped having happy endings, but at some point that's what happened. Maybe that's when you stop being a child, Nick thought. When you realize stories don't always have happy endings. It was like somebody decided you were old enough to be told the truth. "Bad things happen to good people. Deal with it." *I can deal with it,* he thought, *but I'll take a happy ending over a downer every single time.*

Sherry was at her locker when Nick came out of the classroom. He was glad they were back on speaking terms again, but they hadn't talked about the one thing they should be talking about. He knew Sherry was waiting for him to bring it up. So far he'd avoided the subject like the plague, but it was time to man up.

He took a deep breath as he approached her. "A penny for your thoughts," he said. Sherry smiled at him. She had a great smile. The greatest.

"Is that all they're worth?"

"I'm willing to go as high as a dime, but they better be good."

"The last of the big time spenders."

Nick laughed. *Might as well get right to it,* he thought. "I was wondering if you'd like to go for a coffee some time," he said, "and talk about what happened between us."

"I'd like that," she said softly.

"How about Delaney's?" he asked. It was their café. Sherry liked to claim ownership of their favorite places. Delaney's was "Our Café." The park at the bottom of 15th Street was "Our Park," and the picnic table overlooking the water was "Our Table."

"I can't go now," Sherry said. "I have to go to work."

"Where are you working?"

"Aritizia, at Park Royal. I've been working there since the summer."

"I'm surprised I've never seen you. I'm there all the time."

"Really?" Sherry's eyes widened. "When did you start wearing women's clothes?"

Nick laughed. "I meant at the mall." *She knew that, you idiot.* "What time do you finish work?"

"Nine, but I'm meeting a friend after." Nick wondered if her friend was Joe College. "I could meet you tomorrow morning," she suggested. "I don't start work until one."

"That's no good for me," Nick said. He decided not to tell her he was going to the prison to visit his father. He knew she'd be sympathetic, but he didn't want her sympathy—not unless he could have the rest of her as well.

"Then how about Sunday?" she suggested. "My shift ends at five."

"That's no good either. We've got a practice."

"This is getting ridiculous. Tell you what. I'll have my people call your people to set something up."

Nick laughed. "How about Monday? I have a math exam in the morning, but I could meet you after."

"That works for me. I have French in the morning, then I'm free until three when I go to work."

"Great. I'll meet you here."

"Sounds good." She looked at her watch. "Got to run. See you Monday, Nick. Have a great weekend."

"You too." Sherry nodded, and walked away from him. She turned at the end of the hall and called back to him. "Hey Macklin! Keep your elbows up when you go into the corners." A chill went down Nick's spine as she disappeared from sight. Macklin. It had been a long time since she called him that.

CHAPTER TWENTY-FIVE

"Heading out?" Al asked as Nick came downstairs.

Nick took his coat from the closet by the door. "Yeah," he said. "Say hello to everybody for me." He tried to paste a regretful look on his face, as if he was sorry he had to miss Sunday dinner. In fact, he didn't have to miss it now that McAndrew had moved the practice up to three-thirty. But Al didn't need to know that. The last thing Nick wanted to do was sit around the table, pretending everything was hunky-dory, especially when he knew that Al was lying to Helen about his gambling. Anyway, he had more important things to do. The early practice meant he'd be able to get to the mall by the time Sherry finished her shift, instead of having to wait until tomorrow the way they'd arranged.

"How's everything going?" Al asked.

"Good."

"You sure? You've been a little, I don't know, distant the past few weeks."

"I'm fine. Just busy, that's all." Al searched Nick's face. Nick held his gaze, trying not to give anything away.

"Exams must be coming up soon."

"First one's tomorrow."

"Are you ready?"

"I think so," Nick said.

"How's the team looking?"

"We're starting to come together."

"It's good you're playing again."

"Yeah." Nick said as he stepped outside.

He couldn't for the life of him understand why Al was gambling again. On an intellectual level, he knew that an addiction was a disease. But that didn't make it any easier to accept that Al was doing this to Helen. Nick knew Al loved her. Loved her a lot. So why was he doing the one thing that would destroy that love? *I don't care if Al has a disease,* Nick said to himself. *He needs to get his act together.*

McAndrew's message to Lipton after the Ridge Meadow game had apparently gone in one ear and out the other. He was on cruise control for the entire practice—just like he'd been during the team's 5–2 loss to Hollyburn earlier in the week—rousing himself only when a goal-scoring opportunity presented itself. Whenever his team lost possession of the puck, he turned around in lazy circles, trailing the play, and giving the red team one scoring chance after another.

Midway through the scrimmage, McAndrew had finally seen enough. He blew his whistle, stopping the play. "Lipton," he bellowed. "Get over here." Lipton nonchalantly skated over to the coach. McAndrew was fuming. "I've had it up to here with you. Everybody else is busting a gut while you're farting around like you're on a Sunday skate with your grandmother. You don't deserve to wear the same uniform as the rest of these guys."

Nick looked at Red. He could read his mind. *About effing time.*

"You don't care about the other guys on the team. All you care about is Kenny Lipton. You know what I think? I think you should hand in your uniform. You know why?

Because that's a hockey uniform and you're not a hockey player. You think you're a hockey player, but you're not. You don't have it here." McAndrew slapped his heart. "So why don't you do everybody a favor, yourself included, and pack it in." He stared at Lipton. "What are you waiting for?" he demanded. "Go on over there and give Google your uniform." Lipton didn't budge. "What are you waiting for?" McAndrew repeated. "You're keeping the hockey players waiting."

"I'm not quitting," Lipton said, locking eyes with the coach.

"We'll see about that. Give me ten," McAndrew said, pointing at the ice. Lipton got down on the ice and did ten push-ups. "Ten more," said McAndrew. Lipton gave him ten more. "Again." Four sets later Lipton could barely stand. Nick looked over at Red. He was enjoying this.

"Had enough?" McAndrew said. Lipton shook his head. McAndrew skated to one end of the rink, gesturing for Lipton to follow him. The rest of the players stood along the boards as McAndrew put Lipton through suicide drill after suicide drill. Following each one, he asked Lipton if he was ready to quit. Lipton shook his head every time. It was like the two of them were up on a stage, and Nick and the rest of the team were sitting in the audience.

After he'd done six sets—Nick had never seen anybody do more than four—Red skated over to Nick. "You got to hand it to the prick. He's a tough son-of-a-bitch." There was a note of admiration in his voice.

Midway through his eighth set, Lipton was so tired that he couldn't come to a stop. He crashed into the boards and fell onto the ice. McAndrew skated over to him. "Just say the word." Lipton shook his head. He struggled to his knees, using his stick to support himself. He got halfway up before collapsing back on the ice. Nick had never seen anything like it: none of them had. Lipton got on his knees again, crawled to the boards, and pulled himself to his feet. He staggered toward the blue line but before he got there he spun out of control and fell to the ice. This time he didn't get up.

"Practice Tuesday at six," McAndrew said. He skated to the bench, opened the gate, and stepped off the ice. Ivan skated over to Lipton and helped him to his feet. Lipton put one arm around Ivan's shoulder and the other around Josh Parry's. As the two of them helped Lipton off the ice, Red started clapping. The rest of the team joined in.

Nick waited impatiently at the bus stop. He looked at his watch. 4:45. If the bus didn't come in the next couple of minutes, Sherry would be gone by the time he arrived at the mall. He was holding lilies in his left hand. He had bought them on an impulse at the shop across from the arena. Now he wondered if they were a mistake.

"You can never go wrong giving flowers to a girl," his mother once told him. She adored flowers. One of his strongest memories of his mother was of her working in the garden, tending to her flowers. There was always a fresh bouquet on the dinner table.

He gave flowers to Sherry the first time they went out. Surprised the hell out of her. "Nobody's ever given me flowers before," she said, when he handed them to her. When he took her home, she thanked him again. "Lilies are my favorite," she said.

"I'll remember that for next time," he said.

"What makes you think there's going to be a next time?" she asked, standing on the porch with a hand on her hip.

The question had flustered him. He didn't know her well enough to know she was joking. "I just thought … "

"It's okay, Macklin," she said. "I'm just playing with your head. I'd love to go out with you again."

A man and a woman walked by, holding hands. The woman looked at the flowers and gave him a smile. Just then the bus turned the corner and pulled up at the stop. Nick grabbed hold of his hockey bag and got on.

He found a seat, took out his cellphone, and called Ivan. He had rushed off right after practice so they hadn't had a chance to talk about what happened with Lipton.

"Hey."

"That was something else," Nick said.

"Brutal."

"Lipton's a lot tougher than I thought."

"Tougher than I thought too," Ivan said. "Do you think McAndrew was hoping he'd quit?"

"Nah," Nick said. "If he didn't want him around, he would have just kicked him off the team. I think it was a test to find out if Lipton really wanted to play."

"He found out. I didn't know hockey was that important to Lipton."

"He might not have known it himself."

"Maybe that's why McAndrew did it. Not so he could find out if Lipton wanted to play, but so that Lipton would realize how much it meant to him."

"Think it worked?" Nick asked. "Think he'll commit to the team?"

"He knows if he doesn't, McAndrew will give him the boot. And he'll have gone through all that for nothing."

"I hope you're right. If he commits, we've got a real good shot at winning the championship."

"That's the truth, brother. Okay. I gotta run. See you at school tomorrow."

"Later."

The bus hadn't moved in a while. Nick looked out the window and saw a stalled tractor-trailer in the intersection. He looked at his watch. Five to five. He grabbed his bag and hurried to the front of the bus. "I have to get off," he said to the driver.

Nick ran the two blocks to Park Royal, carrying the flowers in his left hand and dragging his hockey bag with his right. He wasn't sure if Aritzia was in the North Mall or the South Mall. He took a chance on the South Mall, and headed toward the entrance. The mall directory was displayed on a console just inside the door. *Shit!* Aritzia was in the North Mall. He raced out the door.

When he got to the store he hurried up to the girl behind the cash. She had a butterfly tattoo on the side of her neck. "Is Sherry here?" he asked.

"She just left."

"Do you know where she went?"

"You can try the café. Turn left at the top of the escalator."

Nick left the store and stepped onto the escalator. A young guy and his girlfriend were coming down on the other side. The girl had her head buried in her boyfriend's chest. He had his arms wrapped around her, his chin rested on her head and his eyes were closed, a blissful look on his face. Looking at them made Nick feel lonely. As he and the young couple were about to pass each other, the girl turned her head to the side and looked in his direction.

It was Sherry.

Nick felt like he'd been punched in the stomach. He turned around after they passed each other and looked back down the escalator. Sherry was looking at him over her boyfriend's shoulder, a pleading, helpless look on her face. The letters *UBC* were sewn on the back of her boyfriend's leather jacket. Nick stared back, stone-faced, then turned away from her. When he got to the top of the escalator, he crammed the flowers into a garbage can. Then he turned around. Sherry was coming up the escalator. She walked up to him.

"What are you doing here?" she asked. She glanced at the flowers in the garbage can.

"No big deal," he said. "They were on sale."

"I'm sorry you had to find out like this."

Nick shrugged. "No big deal," he said again.

Sherry turned and looked back toward the escalator. Joe College was standing at the bottom. He was tall and skinny. He tapped his watch impatiently.

"I have to go," Sherry said.

"So I see. Better run along."

Sherry ignored the taunt. "Let's meet tomorrow, okay? The way we planned."

"What's the problem? Joe College not measuring up?" Nick knew he was being a dick, but he didn't really care.

"Don't be like that."

"Like what? I just want to know that he's giving you a good time—if you know what I mean."

Sherry gave him a disgusted look. "He is," she said. "The best ever."

She went back down the escalator to where Joe College was waiting. He put his arm around her shoulder as they headed off. Sherry put her hand in his back pocket. *That was for me,* Nick thought. He watched the two of them until they disappeared from sight.

CHAPTER TWENTY-SIX

"Pens down," said Mr. Robb, the math teacher.

The exam was harder than Nick expected, but he was satisfied with the way it went. It was a good thing he had woken up early and squeezed in a couple of hours of review in the morning because he hadn't done much studying the night before. After Sherry and her boyfriend left, he had wandered around the mall feeling sorry for himself. After a while that wore off and he started feeling like the asshole he'd been. He couldn't believe he'd been such a jerk. It wasn't like Sherry had led him on. As far as she knew, they were going to meet on Monday to talk about what happened in the past. Instead, he showed up on Sunday expecting ... expecting what?

He knew damn well what he expected. All weekend long he'd imagined how their conversation would go. First he'd tell her how sorry he was for the way he'd treated her. He'd explain he was so messed up after what happened to his dad that he couldn't think straight. He'd tell her that a day didn't go by that he didn't beat himself up for screwing everything up. He'd say that she was the best thing that ever happened to him and he'd tell her that he loved her and that he wanted her back in his life. She'd hear him out, and then she'd forgive him and say that she loved him too: that she'd never stopped loving him.

"I said pens down, Ms. Jenkins."

"I was just … " Emma stuttered, unable to come up with an explanation.

"I was just … I was just … " said Fred Feldman, mocking her.

"Shut up, Fred," Emma said.

"Quiet, you two," Robb ordered. "Leave the exams on your desks."

"When will we get them back, sir?" Emma asked.

"I'll try to get them to you before the holidays."

"Don't hurry on my account, sir," said Fred, as Nick jumped to his feet and raced out of the classroom.

He wasn't surprised that Sherry wasn't at her locker waiting for him, not after last night's performance. He took out his cellphone. He hadn't called her in more than a year but he still knew the number by heart. He punched it in.

"The number you have reached is out of service." It depressed Nick to hear the automated recording. More proof, if more proof was needed, that Sherry had moved on. He pushed through the front door and stepped outside. Sherry was on the sidewalk in front of the school, talking to Vanessa. He should have known she'd be waiting for him. There was no way she was going to let him get away with the things he said.

As he started walking down the stairs, Vanessa saw him coming their way. She tapped Sherry on the shoulder and pointed in his direction. A moment later Sherry was marching toward him with an angry look on her face.

"What the hell is your problem, Macklin?" she said. Hearing her use his last name didn't give him the same charge it usually did. She didn't wait for him to answer. "It's been a year, Nick. What did you think was going to happen? That I was just going to wait around until you were ready to let me back into your life?"

"I'm sorry."

"First you treat me like I don't even exist, like the two years we were together didn't mean a goddamn thing, and then you show up with a bunch of flowers as if that's going to make everything all right. Are you out of your freaking mind?"

Yes, he thought. "I'm sorry," he said again.

"What happened with your dad was horrible. Worse than horrible. But that didn't give you the right to treat me the way you did. I would have been there for you. I *wanted* to be there for you. But you just slammed the door in my face without a word."

"I'm sorry."

"Stop saying that."

"What else can I say? You're right, you're completely right. I was a total jerk. I feel like a real shit, if that makes any difference."

Sherry stared at him for a few seconds. "It helps." The look on her face softened. Nick couldn't think of anything to say except "I'm sorry" so he didn't say anything. "You owe me a coffee," she said finally. "If you still want to talk, that is."

"Absolutely," Nick said with an enthusiasm he didn't feel. He knew the conversation wasn't going to have the happy ending he'd fantasized about. It was just going to remind him of what he'd lost.

"How about Delaney's?" Sherry asked.

Our Café. "Sure," he said, although he'd rather they went somewhere else, somewhere without the memories.

"How was your exam?" she asked as they headed off.

"Not bad. How about yours?"

"It was all right. I'll be glad when they're over," she said.

"Me too. You going to your grandmother's for Christmas?" he asked. Sherry nodded. She always went to her grandmother's on Salt Spring Island for the holidays. "Your dad coming up?" he asked. Sherry's parents separated when she was seven, just after Amy was born. Her father was an engineer and worked for a mining company in Argentina but he and Sherry's mother were on good terms, and he usually spent a few days at Salt Spring over the holidays.

"Not this year," Sherry said. "Dad's too busy. Amy and I are going to visit him during March break. I guess you'll be seeing your father," she said.

"Yeah." He wasn't looking forward to it. He remembered how depressing it had been last Christmas. It was a month after his dad had been convicted, and only the second time Nick had visited him in prison. The prison staff made an attempt to celebrate. There was a Christmas meal with all the trimmings in the gymnasium, presents under a Christmas tree, and a guard dressed up as Santa, but all that did was remind the two of them of how much their lives had changed.

"How is your dad?" Sherry asked.

"He's okay," Nick said with a shrug. They walked along in silence for a while, then Sherry stopped and turned toward him.

"Oh, Nick," she said softly. "It must be so hard for you." Tears welled in her eyes.

"It's okay." He could feel himself starting to choke up.

"I love him too, you know," she said. Tears started streaming down her cheeks. He drew her into his arms and started crying too. They held onto each other fiercely, letting it all out, giving in to their grief over everything they had lost.

"I know it wasn't the same for me as it was for you. Not even close," Sherry said when they finally separated. She wiped away her tears with her sleeve. "But it changed my life too. All these feelings I had—for your dad, for you, for us—I wanted to share them with you, to go through it with you. You didn't give me a chance. I loved you so much," she said. Nick noticed that she used the past tense. "You broke my heart. It took me a long time to get over it."

"I'm sorry," he said. "I know, I know. I've got to stop saying that." Sherry laughed weakly. Then Nick told her everything he'd planned on telling her, everything except how much he missed her and how much he wanted her back in his life. She heard him out, and then she forgave him, just like he knew she would.

"Do you mind if we keep walking?" Nick asked when they got to Delaney's. The last thing he wanted right now was to be surrounded by a bunch of strangers.

"Nice try, Macklin. You owe me a coffee."

"What would you like?"

"A mochachino with extra whipped cream."

"Wait here," Nick said. "I'll be right back." He went inside the café. When he came back with their drinks, Sherry was sitting on a bench on the sidewalk, her thumbs flying over the keyboard of her cellphone. He imagined she was sending Joe College a farewell message. Sorry, Joe. I love Nick. Always have, always will. *Dream on,* he said to himself.

Sherry smiled at him as she put her phone away and got to her feet. They walked to their park at the bottom of 15th Street, sat down at their table, and looked out over the ocean. It felt so right to be with her. In his heart Nick believed she felt the same way he did. But his brain knew otherwise. He could have sat there talking to her forever, but an hour later she had to leave for work. He walked her to the bus stop.

"Do you think we can be friends?" she asked, looking him squarely in the eye.

Nick's heart ached with desire and regret. "Absolutely."

The bus pulled up. Sherry hugged him. "I'll always love you, Nick," she said. The bus door opened. Sherry stepped inside and waved as the bus drove off. *I'll always love you.* He knew she meant it. She just didn't mean it the way he wished she did.

Nick saw his bus coming from the opposite direction and hurried across the street. He got on and put his token in the box.

The bus was almost empty. He walked past an elderly couple sitting at the front. A bald man with a round face sat a few rows behind them. He smiled at Nick as he walked by. Nick noticed that he had a large gap between his front teeth. He took a seat a couple of rows behind the man. It would be easy to forget about a gap between someone's teeth, he thought.

The bus pulled up to Nick's stop. The elderly couple got off, but Nick stayed in his seat. He and the bald man were now the only two passengers on the bus. Two stops later the bald man stood up and pushed the stop request button. Nick got to his feet too. The bald man walked to the front of the bus. He didn't limp. Nick followed him off the bus. He stood for a moment and watched the man stride away, then crossed the street and waited at the bus stop on the other side.

Nick puzzled over one question during the ride back to the house, and he was still chewing it over when he got to his room. It was familiar territory, but if he could answer that one question, he would break the case wide open. *Who else had a motive to murder Marty Albertson?*

There had to be someone who wanted him dead. Nick opened his desk drawer and took out the detective's report. After he finished reading it, he tossed it on his desk. There was something in there, something he was missing. He knew it, but he couldn't put his finger on it. He picked up the report and turned back to page one.

CHAPTER TWENTY-SEVEN

Nick put his physics exam on Mrs. Patel's desk and walked out of the classroom feeling free as a bird. It was his last exam and it felt like the holidays had started, even though there was another week of school left.

Ivan joined him at his locker. "That wasn't too bad," he said.

"At least it's over."

"Happy Birthday, dude. The big one-seven. Getting up there," he said, handing him a gift-wrapped package.

"Thanks," Nick said. Ivan first gave him a birthday present when they were twelve years old. Surprised the hell out of him. It was a Seattle Seahawks jersey. Number 37: Jackie Parker. His favorite player at the time. Nick still had the jersey. From then on, he and Ivan exchanged presents every year. Except this year, Nick remembered guiltily. He didn't give Ivan anything in June when he turned seventeen. Nick was so wrapped up in himself, it hadn't even crossed his mind. Ivan could have used that as an excuse not to get him anything. But he didn't. No surprise there, Nick thought. That's the kind of guy Ivan was.

Nick unwrapped the present. It was a book, *The Boys of Winter,* about the US victory over the Russians in the 1980 Olympics. It was one of the greatest upsets in hockey history. The Russians were expected to win by a landslide, but the Americans shocked the hockey world with a 4–3 victory.

Nick was touched by his friend's thoughtfulness. There was more to the gift than the book itself. He and Ivan had watched *Miracle On Ice,* the movie about the game, with his dad. His father had chosen it for movie night and invited Ivan to watch it with them. The next week his dad borrowed a DVD of the actual game, and the three of them watched that too. Even though he knew who was going to win, it was one of the most exciting games Nick had ever seen.

"If we played them ten times, they might win nine ... " Ivan started.

Nick jumped in. "But not this game. Not tonight. Tonight we are the greatest hockey team in the world." They both laughed. It was a quote from the American coach's pre-game speech. He and Ivan had been using it ever since they saw the movie.

"Want to catch a flick?"

"Can't. I have my road test this afternoon" Nick said, referring to the test for his permanent license. "Got any tips for me?"

"Don't run over anyone. They take a lot of points off when you do that."

"I'll keep that in mind."

"Big game Sunday night," Ivan said. The Lightning had a rematch with Surrey, who had trounced them the last time out. "Payback time."

"I like our chances," Nick said. "Especially with the way Lipton's playing."

"I guess McAndrew knew what he was doing," Ivan said. "It's like Kenny's a different person."

Nick nodded. It was amazing how Lipton had turned things around. His ordeal hadn't ended with the suicide drill. McAndrew had kept on his case all week, just to make sure he got the point. It was clear that he did. Lipton had worked his ass off and kept his mouth shut. It was as if a light bulb had turned on in his head: as if he finally understood how selfish he'd been. It was probably the first time he'd ever been called out, Nick thought. A lot of coaches let their stars get away with shit they wouldn't tolerate in less talented players, but McAndrew wasn't one of them.

Nick closed his locker. He held up the book, and looked at Ivan. "Thanks, man. I really appreciate this."

"No problem." They jabbed fists, then Ivan headed off. Nick opened his locker and grabbed his jacket. He turned on his cellphone. It beeped, indicating he had a text message. He opened it. It was from Sherry.

Happy Birthday ☺

Nick's dad called as he was walking up the front path to the house.

"Happy Birthday, Nick," he said. "How did the exam go?"

"I think it went all right, but you never know."

"I'm sure you did fine. What time is the road test?"

"Four-thirty."

"Make sure you don't drive too fast. Especially if the roads are wet."

"I won't."

"And check your blind spot every time you make a turn or change lanes."

"I will."

"All right. I have to get back to work. The potatoes are waiting." Nick's dad worked in the prison kitchen. "I'll see you the day after tomorrow. Well, happy birthday again. I love you, son."

"I love you too, Dad. See you on Saturday." Nick walked into the house. Helen was sitting on a couch in the living room, reading. Alfie purred at her feet. She picked him up and put him on her lap.

"Happy Birthday, Nick," she said. She handed him an envelope. "This is from your father. And this," she said, handing him another envelope, "is from Al and me."

He opened Al and Helen's present first. It was a gift certificate to HMV. "Thanks Helen," he said, giving her a hug.

"You're welcome."

Nick opened the envelope from his dad and read the card. "Happy birthday to the finest son a man could have. Love, Dad." Inside were two tickets to the Cliques and Friques concert. One of Nick's favorite bands. Sherry's too. At least it used to be.

"How did he get his hands on these?" Nick asked. The concert was three months away, but it had sold out the day tickets went on sale.

"Al pulled a few strings," Helen said. "Oh, my goodness! Is it twelve-thirty already? I'm going to be late for my Pilates class." She put Alfie down and jumped to her feet. "Good luck on your test," she said.

Nick went upstairs to his room. He put the envelope with the concert tickets in his desk drawer. *Maybe Sherry and I will be back together by then,* he couldn't help thinking. *Don't go there,* he warned himself. He decided to invite Google. It would be a nice way to thank him for everything he'd done. He opened his knapsack and took out the book Ivan had given him. The picture on the cover showed the American players celebrating on the ice after the victory.

He flashed on an image of himself, his dad, and his

mom seated on the couch in the den, eating pizza and watching a movie on TV. He was suddenly overwhelmed by sadness. It happened less and less these days—Nick had to admit that he'd been a lot happier during the past three weeks, since he'd stopped looking for Baldy—but it still happened. "Think of it this way," Davis said at their last session. "Imagine that your sadness is stored in one room, instead of being spread all over the house. Now you only have to go into that room once in a while, you don't have to be there all the time."

Nick looked at the book cover again. He didn't enter the room often these days. But he was going there now.

CHAPTER TWENTY-EIGHT

Nick had the familiar pre-game butterflies in his stomach by the time he pulled up in front of the church in North Vancouver on Sunday afternoon. He'd been thinking about the Surrey game all day.

A group of men and women—the members of Al's GA group—was standing on the steps.

"Thanks for the lift," Al said.

"No problem. Thanks for letting me use your car," Nick answered.

"If the province thinks you're qualified to drive by yourself, who am I to disagree?" Al said, shrugging in mock disbelief that Nick had passed his road test. "Who are you playing tonight?"

"Surrey."

"Good luck."

"Thanks," Nick said.

Al got out of the car. Through the rear-view mirror Nick saw him standing on the sidewalk, looking in his direction, as if he were waiting for Nick to drive out of sight.

He's not going to his meeting, Nick said to himself. He decided to follow Al to see where he was really going.

He took the first right, circled back around to East 10ᵗʰ and pulled over to the side of the road. He got out of the car and walked back toward the church. He hid behind a tree and peeked out. He didn't expect to see Al at the church, but there he was, chatting away with the rest of his group. A couple of seconds later the front door opened, and Al and the others walked in.

Nick turned and walked back to the car. He wondered if he'd been wrong about Al. Maybe he hadn't started gambling again. Al always had some kind of business deal happening on the side. That could explain why he gave money to that guy at the Giants game.

Biggie was lifting his hockey bag out of the trunk of his car when Nick pulled into the arena parking lot. He turned into the adjoining space and got out of Al's Lexus.

"They'll give anybody a license these days," Biggie joked.

"I almost didn't pass," Nick said. "I was doing fine until I had to parallel park. I was so paranoid about hitting the curb that it took me four tries to get in. Meanwhile the examiner's going like this on the chart." Nick drew a series of Xs in the air. "I was sure I was going to fail."

Nick popped the trunk and took out his gear. As they walked toward the arena entrance, Biggie's cellphone rang. He flipped it open. "Hey babe," he said, his face lighting up. Nick felt a stab of envy. "I'll catch up to you inside," Biggie said. Nick nodded and entered the arena.

He was near the concession stand when Ivan and Red came through the front door. He stopped to wait for them.

Kenny Lipton and his father were standing in front of the concession stand, talking to a burly guy in a University of Michigan jacket.

"We're losing eight seniors this year," the burly guy said.

"That's a lot of spots to fill," Mr. Lipton said.

"That's why I'm here." *So Lipton's dad managed to get a Michigan scout to come see Kenny play after all,* Nick thought. The server put two cups of coffee on the counter. The scout reached into his pocket but Mr. Lipton put out a hand to stop him.

"On me," he said, as if he was buying the guy a steak dinner. He took out his wallet and handed a bill to the server.

"I see you guys have turned it around," the scout said to Kenny.

"Yeah," Mr. Lipton answered before Kenny could open his mouth. "Kenny's finally getting a little help from some of the role players." He put his arm around his son. Kenny slid out of his grasp, and bent down to tie his shoelace. He glanced up at Nick with an embarrassed look.

"You ready?" Ivan asked Nick as he and Red walked up beside him.

"We are going to kick ass tonight," Red said. One thing about Red, he didn't need a motivational speech to get going. He always came ready to play.

A group of Surrey players stood outside the visitors' locker room. Nick and Jeff Leibel, Surrey's captain, exchanged nods. The two of them had played against each other for years. Nick respected Leibel and the feeling was mutual. During the game they went after each other with no holds barred, but they always left it on the ice. The last time they played, Leibel made a point of coming up to Nick and telling him that he was glad to see him back in uniform.

"Good day, ladies," Red said cheerfully as they walked by the Surrey players. Nick and Ivan looked at each other. Ivan shrugged. Red was Red. There was nothing anybody could do about it.

"Fuck off," a few of the Surrey players said in unison. Red walked past them, his hand in the air, middle finger extended.

Nick was tightening his laces when Kenny Lipton came out of McAndrew's office, a pained expression on his face. The coach emerged a few seconds later.

"Listen up," he said. The room quieted down. McAndrew had a number of different pre-game speeches that he used to motivate the team. His choice depended on the situation. Today he used a variation of the non-motivational motivational speech.

"All right men. There's no point in my telling you what this game means. Or what it's going to take to beat Surrey. If you don't know by now, we're in deep trouble. They're big and they're tough and they're going to be intense from the get-go. We're going to have to match that intensity, or we'll be in for a long night." His eyes swept over the players, one by one. "Okay, bring it in."

The players gathered around him. They put their sticks in the middle of the circle. "One, Two, Three—Lightning!"

Halfway through the first period, Nick understood why Lipton had a pained expression on his face when he left McAndrew's office. He hadn't gotten off the bench and it was obvious he wasn't going to. The coach was putting him through one last test. So far Kenny was acing it. It didn't take much imagination to realize that it must be killing him not to be out on the ice, especially with the Michigan scout in the stands. But Kenny had kept his feelings in check and yelled himself hoarse, cheering for his teammates from his spot on the bench.

It was a tight defensive battle from the opening faceoff.

Neither team could generate a good scoring opportunity. Nick's battle with Leibel was as intense as ever, neither one giving the other any breathing room. It was as if they were stuck together with Krazy Glue. With three minutes left in the second period, Ed Bradley banged in a rebound off Josh Parry's shot from the point, giving the Lightning a 1–0 lead.

"Way to hustle," Kenny said to Nick, slapping him on the shoulder pads as they walked toward the locker room for the ten-minute intermission between the second and third periods.

"Hang in there," Nick said.

Lipton's father was waiting outside the locker room. He stepped in front of McAndrew as he was about to go in. "What the hell is going on?" he asked. "Why isn't Kenny playing?"

"I'm not going to talk about this now," McAndrew said. "We can discuss it after the game."

"You listen to me, McAndrew." Mr. Lipton was fuming. "There's a scout from the University of Michigan here. He didn't come all this way to see Kenny sit on the bench." Nick glanced at Kenny. He was staring at the floor, as though he wished it would open and swallow him up.

"I already told you, Mr. Lipton," McAndrew said calmly, "I'm not going to get into this now. Come see me after the game."

"You're damn well going to talk to me now," said Lipton's dad, glaring at McAndrew. McAndrew stared back at him. After a few seconds, Lipton's dad looked away. "You haven't heard the end of this," he snarled before he stalked away.

Cliff Henry's empty net goal gave the Lightning a 2-0

victory, but to nobody's surprise, McAndrew kept Lipton on the bench for the rest of the game. His teammates made a point of coming up to him in the locker room after the game, to say a few words or tap him on the shin pads in a gesture of support. He'd earned a lot of respect by the way he'd gutted it out during the suicide drills, and a lot more by the way he'd handled being benched.

Red wheeled his bag past Nick's locker. "See you at Mike's," he said. Nick nodded. Red stopped in front of Lipton. He was still wearing his uniform. "See you at practice tomorrow, Kenny," he said.

"See you, Red."

"Great game, Red," Josh Parry said, as Red passed by his locker. He held out his hand, and Red slapped it.

"You too, big guy," Red said.

Nick caught Ivan's eye. He knew they were both thinking the same thing. The team was finally coming together.

Lipton was still in his uniform when Nick left. "See you, Kenny," he said.

"Later."

Nick walked through the deserted arena and out the front door. He felt a chill go through him. The cold spell had lasted all week, but he still wasn't used to it. Where was global warming when you needed it? He reached into his jacket pockets but his gloves weren't there so he went back into the arena to see if he'd left them in the locker room.

As he neared the locker room, Nick heard Mr. Lipton's voice booming from inside. "Why didn't you tell me you were in McAndrew's doghouse? If I'd known, I wouldn't have broken my balls getting Michigan to send a scout here to watch you play. Do you have any idea how embarrassing that was for me? The idea was for you to get a hockey scholarship, sport, not a cheerleading scholarship. How could you do this to me?"

The door to the dressing room burst open. Lipton's dad stomped out. He glared at Nick. "What are you looking at?" he said as he stormed off.

Nick went into the dressing room. Lipton didn't look up. He was slumped in his chair, staring at the wall. Nick spotted his gloves on the floor by his locker. He picked them up and put them in his pocket. He glanced over at Kenny. Kenny continued to stare at the wall, then he shifted his gaze to Nick.

"I hate his guts. I hate his freaking guts."

It was past eleven by the time the guys left Mike's Diner. Nick got behind the wheel of the Lexus, put on his seat belt, and started the engine. He and his friends had spent most of the time talking about what an asshole Lipton's dad was. Nick didn't tell the guys about the scene he'd overhead in the locker room. He wished he hadn't heard it himself, he felt like he'd been slimed.

Nick had seen lots of crazed parents in the years he'd played hockey: the ones who were always yelling at their kids, dissing other people's kids, and blaming the coach when things didn't go well. Away from the arena they were normal, but once the puck was dropped, it was like aliens invaded their bodies. But he'd never seen anyone like Kenny Lipton's dad.

Nick remembered the look on Kenny's face when his father confronted McAndrew outside the dressing room. It never occurred to Mr. Lipton how that was going to make his son feel. There were a lot of adults like that, Nick thought. They didn't seem to understand that kids had thoughts and feelings of their own, or if they did they didn't think they mattered. They demanded you respect them, not because they'd done anything to earn it, but because they were older. Like that was some kind of fantastic achievement. It was as if they woke up one morning, decided they were all grown up, and then pushed a button that erased all memory of what it felt like to be a kid.

Dr. Davis had told Nick that boys look to their fathers to show them how to be men. No wonder Kenny had been so selfish. Look at the example he grew up with.

Nick drove out of the parking lot and turned onto Marine Drive. Up ahead in the next block, he saw the flashing lights of a police cruiser. He slowed down as he approached it. The cruiser was parked on an angle, its front wheels on the sidewalk. Two cops were leading someone around the front of the cruiser. As they stepped out onto the street, they were caught in the glare of Nick's headlights. Nick's eyes nearly popped out of his head. He looked into the rear-view mirror as he passed, pulled over to the curb, and took out his cellphone. Then he called Ivan and told him that Kenny Lipton had just been arrested by the West Vancouver police.

CHAPTER TWENTY-NINE

Putnam walked up and down the aisles handing out a reading list. "If you want to choose a book that's not on the list, that's fine," he said, "but you'll have to clear it with me first."

Nick checked the time. Two minutes until the bell. He glanced at Ivan. Ivan nodded. The two of them were going to McAndrew's office after class to tell him about Lipton's arrest and see if he could find out what happened.

"It's not fair to give us homework over the holidays, sir," Zoe Taylor said.

"You don't have to write anything. You just have to read the book and choose an essay topic by the time school starts. That's not homework by my definition."

"When are we getting our exams back, sir?" asked Emma Jenkins.

"Not until January, but you'll have your report cards on Friday."

"They just do that so we'll come to school on Friday," Jason Turner said.

"Correct," said Putnam.

The bell rang. Nick and Ivan hurried out of the classroom.

"I haven't seen you in a while, Nick," said Mrs. Lewis. "What can I do for you?"

"We'd like to see Mr. McAndrew," Nick answered.

Mrs. Lewis picked up the phone and asked the VP if he was free. "Go right in," she said, waving her hand in the direction of McAndrew's office.

"I don't believe it," McAndrew said, leaning back in his chair. "Do you know what he was arrested for?"

Nick shook his head. McAndrew reached for his agenda and leafed through it. "I have a friend in the police department," he said. He picked up his phone and punched in the number. "Detective Flynn, please. Ray, it's Jack McAndrew here ... Fine, but listen. A kid on my team was picked up by a couple of your guys last night around eleven. Can you find out what happened? ... Kenneth Lipton ... L-I-P-T-O-N ... I'll be here. Thanks."

McAndrew hung up. "He's going to call me right back." He shook his head. "I thought Kenny finally had his act together." Nick was about to tell him about the scene in the locker room when the phone rang.

"Jack McAndrew ... Yeah ... uh-huh ... okay ... His dad didn't come for him until this morning? ... He's a real jerk. I had a run-in with him during the game because I benched his son ... Kenny's a good kid. He just needs some discipline. What's going to happen now? ... Great ... Thanks Ray, I owe you one." McAndrew put the receiver down.

"Lipton smashed in some store windows with his hockey stick. He was charged with mischief, but seeing as he's a minor and has never been in trouble with the law before, the charges will be dropped. He'll probably have to do some community service."

Nick thought it was funny that they called it mischief. When his mom used to tell him not to get into any mischief, she was referring to things like writing on the wall with his crayons, not smashing a window. She'd have used a stronger word for that.

"Did Kenny spend the night in jail?" Ivan asked.

McAndrew nodded. "His father told the police to keep him overnight to 'teach him a lesson.'" He drew quotation marks in the air.

"What a prick," Nick blurted out. McAndrew nodded in agreement.

"Do you guys have any idea why Kenny did this?" McAndrew asked.

"I do," Nick said. He told McAndrew about how Lipton's dad had berated him in the locker room. It made Nick angry just thinking about it. He could see it made McAndrew angry as well.

"That's horrible," he said, "but it doesn't justify what Kenny did. He's not a baby anymore. He has to take responsibility for himself."

"Are you going to kick him off the team?" Nick asked.

"What do you guys think I should do?"

"You know how much hockey means to him," Nick said. "He shouldn't have to lose that because he broke a few windows. It's not like he did something really serious." *He was just up to some mischief,* he thought, but he kept that thought to himself.

"He broke the law. I'd say that was pretty serious."

"Everybody deserves a second chance," Ivan said.

"I already gave him a second chance."

"Yeah. And he changed. You saw how he changed."

"You both seem to feel pretty strongly about this," McAndrew said. Nick and Ivan nodded. "I won't make a decision until I've spoken with him. He's going to have to convince me that he can control himself. Fair enough?"

Nick and Ivan nodded again.

"Good. See you guys at practice tomorrow." They stood up to leave. "Hang on, Nick. Could I speak to you for a moment?"

"I'll catch up to you later," Nick said to Ivan.

McAndrew waited for the door to close, then he took an envelope out of his desk and handed it Nick. "It's your report card. I'm not supposed to show it to you until Friday, but here it is."

Nick opened the envelope. 81 in English; 77 in Math; 78 in Biology; 75 in Chemistry; 76 in Physics. Nick couldn't believe it. He knew he'd done well, but he didn't think he'd done this well.

"Congratulations," McAndrew said with a smile. "You deserve a lot of credit for the way you turned things around. I'm proud of you."

"Thanks." Nick suddenly realized that McAndrew's opinion mattered to him. It was quite a difference from the way he felt the day he asked the coach if he could rejoin the team. It was hard to believe that was only a month and a half ago. He knew McAndrew wasn't the one who had changed.

Nick put his report card back in the envelope and handed it to McAndrew. As the coach took it, Nick looked at the framed picture of McAndrew in his hockey uniform, back when he had a full head of hair. The team name was written across his chest. The Kingston Frontenacs. A chill went through Nick's body. Marty Albertson had played for the Kingston Frontenacs too. Until he was in that car accident. The one that injured two of his teammates.

CHAPTER THIRTY

They didn't call him Google for nothing. He'd been on the computer for less than two minutes when he called Nick over. "Here it is," he said, pointing to a headline from an article in the Kingston Whig Standard. TWO FRONTENACS INJURED IN LATE NIGHT JOY RIDE.

"Holy shit!" Nick said when he was partway through the article.

"Yeah," Google agreed solemnly.

McAndrew was one of the two players who were injured when Albertson drove the car off the road, but that's not why Nick's heart was beating so quickly. He'd already figured that out. It was the identity of the second passenger that took him by surprise. *Colin* McAndrew, the coach's twin brother. According to the newspaper article, his spinal cord had been severed. The doctors said he would never walk again.

"What do you think?" Google asked. He didn't wait for Nick to answer. "Albertson ends McAndrew's career, puts his brother in a wheelchair, and walks away without a scratch. People have killed for less."

It made sense to Nick, until he thought about it for a moment. "We're forgetting one thing," he said. "This happened nine years ago. If McAndrew was going to kill Albertson, why would he wait so long?"

"I don't know. But you have to admit it's a helluva

140

coincidence," Google said as he typed "Colin McAndrew" in the search box and hit the return key.

"That's all it is. A coincidence," Nick said with a shrug.

"I guess this is just a coincidence too?" Google said triumphantly. Nick looked at the computer screen.

"McAndrew, Colin Edward. Passed away on Tuesday, September 15 at St. Paul's Hospital. Survived by his mother, Margaret, his brother, Jack and his sister, Christine. A private family service will be held. In lieu of flowers, donations to the Canadian Paraplegic Association would be appreciated."

September 15. Two days before Albertson was killed. Could Colin's death have been enough to push McAndrew over the edge? Could it have been a motive for murder?

Google tapped away on his computer. "Hold on," he said. "Albertson died between four and seven, right?" Nick nodded. He looked at the computer screen. Google had called up the team's schedule from last season. "Then McAndrew couldn't have done it," Google said. "We had a practice from 4:30 to 6:30. It would have taken McAndrew an hour to drive from Albertson's condo to the rink."

"Maybe he wasn't at the practice," Nick suggested. It didn't happen often, but it happened.

"Don't think so," Google said. "Look." He pointed to the calendar box for September 17, the day Albertson was murdered. The words *Team Picture* were written inside. Google gestured toward the bulletin board above the computer. The team picture from last year was pinned to it. And there was McAndrew, sitting right in the middle of the front row.

Nick stood at the bus stop. He was both disappointed and relieved that McAndrew had nothing to do with

Albertson's death. It would have been terrible if he had been involved. But it put an end to his short-lived fantasy that he could finally prove that his father was innocent.

He checked his watch. It was just after six. Dinnertime at the prison. His dad would be sitting at a table in his prison-issued blue jeans and white T-shirt, indistinguishable from all the other men in jeans and T-shirts. His father never talked about what it was like to be in jail, and Nick never asked. But one day when he was waiting for his dad in the visiting room, he heard another prisoner complain about the routine.

"Wake up at six. Head count. Breakfast at seven. Head count at eleven. Lunch at noon. Head count at five. Dinner at six. Head count at ten. Lights out at eleven. The next day you get up and do it all over again. Day after day after day. It's been eight months and I'm going out of my mind. I don't know if I can handle three more years of this." Nick had wanted to strangle the guy. *Three years! Try twenty-five, dickhead.*

CHAPTER THIRTY-ONE

Nick closed his locker, clicked the combination lock shut, and spun the dial a couple of times. The hallways were buzzing with excitement. There was still one more day of school, but everybody was already in holiday mode.

Sherry was standing at her locker. She turned and saw Nick looking at her. She was wearing another one of her T-shirts: KEEP THE EARTH CLEAN. IT'S NOT URANUS. She gave him a smile, as he walked up beside her.

"Hey," she said.

"Hey."

They headed down the hallway together. Fred Feldman and Emma Jenkins were standing near the front door, talking away like the best of friends.

"See you tomorrow," Nick said.

"You won't be seeing me, dude," said Fred. "They're expecting twelve inches of fresh poop at Whistler. F squared is officially on holiday."

"You're such a bad boy," Emma said sarcastically.

"Look who's talking," Fred said. "You're probably going to come to school during the holidays."

"I would, if I wasn't going to be blowing by you on the Couloir." Nick looked at Emma in surprise. He wouldn't have figured she would know the name of one of the toughest runs at Whistler, let alone be able to ski down it. Fred must have felt the same way, judging by the wide-eyed look on his face. For the first time in his life he didn't have a quick comeback.

"Now there's something I didn't think I'd ever see," Nick said to Sherry as they walked into the sunshine.

"Why? It's obvious they like each other."

"I guess," Nick said. "When are you going to Salt Spring?" he asked.

"Saturday."

"If I don't see you at school tomorrow, have a great holiday."

"You too." Nick watched Sherry walk across the street to the bus stop. An all too familiar feeling of loss swept over him. He remembered how she once told him that she couldn't understand people who didn't remain friends after they broke up. It might take time, she said, but if they really cared about each other, they'd end up being friends. "Promise me we'll always be friends, no matter what," she had said to him. He promised. It didn't occur to him that they would ever be apart. Sherry was talking to a classmate as she waited at the bus stop. It hurt just to look at her. *Sherry and I can be friends,* Nick thought, *as long as we don't actually spend any time together.*

Nick headed for the school parking lot. Helen had gone to a yoga retreat in California and had given him her car for the week. He had a couple of hours to kill before practice. He decided to go to Mike's Diner and finish reading the book he'd chosen from Putnam's list. It was about Rubin "Hurricane" Carter, an American boxer who'd been wrongly convicted of murder and spent nearly twenty years in jail before he was freed. Nick wondered if Putnam had been thinking of him when he put the book on the reading list.

Nick closed the book and put it on the table. Then he picked it up again and turned back to the page he'd folded over. He reread the paragraph he'd underlined. It was what Rubin Carter said at a press conference after he was finally released from prison. *The most productive years of my life, between the ages of twenty-nine and fifty, have been stolen, the fact that I was deprived of seeing my children grow up—wouldn't you think I have a right to be bitter? Wouldn't anyone under those circumstances have a right to be bitter? In fact, it would be very easy to be bitter. But it has never been my nature, or my lot, to do things the easy way. If I have learned nothing else in my life, I've learned that bitterness only consumes the vessel that contains it. And for me to permit bitterness to control or to infect my life in any way whatsoever, would be to allow those who imprisoned me to take even more than the twenty-two years they've already taken.*

His dad hadn't used the same words, but that's what he'd been trying to tell Nick all along. They had taken away his freedom. All he had left was his humanity. He wasn't going to let them have that too.

A rapping on the window interrupted Nick's thoughts. Kenny Lipton was standing outside the diner. He motioned to indicate he was coming inside. Nick watched Lipton walk around to the entrance to the diner, pulling his hockey bag behind him. *Excellent,* Nick thought. *McAndrew has let him stay on the team.*

Lipton smiled at Nick as he walked over to his booth. "Hey."

"How's it going?"

"McAndrew told me that you and Ivan put in a good word for me. Thanks. I really appreciate it," Kenny said.

"No big deal. Everybody on the team feels the same way. Did he give you a hard time?"

"He was pretty good about it, but he made it clear that

if I screw up again, I'm gone. I guess you could say I'm on probation," Lipton said with a rueful grin.

"McAndrew said the cops were going to drop the charges."

"Yeah. I have to do a hundred hours of community service, serving food to the homeless. And I have to do work around the house to pay my dad back for the windows."

Things must be pretty tense in the Lipton household, Nick thought. The worst thing he had ever done was to steal some CDs from Future Shop. The store manager called the police. Nick's dad was at the front door when they brought him home. His father didn't lose his temper, but Nick almost wished he had. Anything would have been better than that look of disappointment on his face.

"McAndrew said you saw the cops arresting me," Lipton said.

"Yeah. I saw them putting you in the cruiser. Freaked me right out."

"You heard what my dad said to me in the locker room, right?" Lipton asked. Nick nodded. He didn't think he'd ever forget it. "The last thing I wanted to do was go home. I started walking down Marine Drive. All of a sudden I'm standing in front of a store, only instead of seeing my reflection in the window I see my dad's. Next thing I know there's glass all over the sidewalk, and the store alarm is going off. And then the cops show up. You know the rest."

"Coach said you spent the night in jail."

"My dad thought it would teach me a lesson."

"It must have been scary."

"It was. They put me in a holding cell with two other guys. All I could think about was the stuff you see on TV."

Lipton didn't have to spell it out. "As soon as we started talking," he went on, "I could see they were harmless. One guy was in there for drunk driving, and the other had been caught shoplifting. But I didn't get a lot of sleep … I guess we should head over to the arena, or we'll be late for practice."

Nick nodded and stood up. He thought about asking Kenny how things were going at home but he was pretty sure he knew the answer to that one.

The locker room buzzed with energy after practice. Nobody was in a hurry to go home. They were all looking forward to Hollyburn's annual Christmas tournament. It was one of the biggest events of the season and the best teams in the province would be there.

McAndrew appeared in the doorway. "With a little work, you guys might actually turn out to be a half decent hockey team," he said. Coming from McAndrew, that was glowing praise. "Of course, it helps to have guys as buff as Biggie and Josh," he continued, drawing everybody's attention to the pair of them. They both had their shirts off; their bellies hung over their hockey pants. It didn't mean they were out of shape. When you were that big, it was next to impossible to have a flat stomach. Everybody laughed.

"There's a six-pack under here, Coach," Biggie said. "You just can't see it."

"The only six-pack you'll ever have is at the beer store," McAndrew said. Everybody laughed again. "Okay. Listen up. We practice Sunday and Monday at three. Then we're off until the tournament. Our first game is Thursday against Kamloops. I don't know what time, but we'll email the schedule to you as soon as we get it. See you Sunday," he said, as he limped out of the room.

"I wish the tournament was starting tomorrow," Ivan said to Nick.

"Me too." Nick looked around the room. Everybody was smiling and laughing. It was a complete turnaround from the way things had been when he rejoined the team. It had been tough going, but they had finally gotten their act together.

"I like our chances," Ivan said.

Nick looked across the room to where Lipton was unlacing his skates. Whatever shit Kenny might be dealing with at home, he hadn't brought it out on the ice with him. He had dominated the scrimmage from start to finish. *If Kenny plays like that in the tournament,* Nick thought, *I like our chances too. I like them a lot.*

Nick drove out of the arena parking lot and turned right on Marine Drive. He was still thinking about the tournament. He'd never played on a team that had won it, and this would be his last chance.

He turned onto 15th Street and headed up to the highway. Two police cars were parked in the driveway of a house at the corner. The scene reminded Nick of the night his father was arrested. Mr. Caldwell, the photographer who had taken the team picture, gave him a lift home after practice that day. They had just turned onto Nick's street when he saw two police cars, lights flashing, parked in their driveway. Nick hadn't given it a second thought. They'd been having trouble with their house alarm, and he figured it had gone off by accident again. Then the front door opened, and his father came out of the house, escorted by four policemen. When Nick ran up to his dad, he saw the handcuffs.

Wait a minute, he thought. *According to the schedule on Google's computer, the team picture was taken on September 17—the day Albertson was killed. That's why we figured McAndrew couldn't have been involved in the murder. But Dad was arrested on September 18. If Caldwell drove me home on the 18ᵗʰ, the team picture must have been taken the day after Albertson was killed.*

Ten minutes later Nick was in front of Google's computer. "Here it is," Google said. Nick leaned over his shoulder and read the email.

"Practice on Tuesday, September 17 is cancelled. Team pictures will be taken after practice on the 18th."

Nick and Google stared at each other in disbelief. McAndrew's alibi had just gone up in smoke.

CHAPTER THIRTY-TWO

It was 4:40. Nick had been hiding in the toilet stall since two-thirty, when school ended. He opened the door and walked to the washroom window. His legs were cramped from sitting so long. It was the last day of school before the holidays and the teachers had all left early. The only vehicle in the parking lot was the pickup truck belonging to one of the janitors. He would be working at the school all night. He and Google would have to gamble that they could get in and out of McAndrew's office without his seeing them.

Nick tapped lightly on the stall next to the one he'd been in. "Let's go," he whispered. Google emerged, and the two of them walked to the washroom door. Nick was just about to open it when a creaking sound came from the hallway. He and Google hurried back into their stalls.

Nick squatted on the toilet seat, his feet off the ground. He heard the door to the washroom open. Through the crack in the door he saw the janitor in his blue uniform come in, pulling a creaky mop and bucket behind him. The janitor moved out of Nick's line of sight. Nick heard the slap of the mop on the floor, followed by a squishing sound as the janitor cleaned the floor. *Slap. Slap. Squish. Squish.* The wheels creaked as the bucket rolled toward the toilet stalls. Nick prayed that the janitor was too lazy to wash the floor inside the stalls.

His prayer went unanswered. The door to the adjoining

stall banged open. *Slap. Slap. Squish. Squish.* His heart was pounding. *We're screwed,* Nick thought. The mop strayed into Nick's stall. His heart pounded harder as he stared at the mop in horror. *F-u-u-u-c-k,* he said to himself.

The janitor's cellphone rang. "Hello. Yes, sir," he said in a high-pitched voice. "There's one in the storage room. I'll put it outside your office … No problem." Nick heard the janitor walk out of the washroom, leaving the mop and bucket behind. As soon as the door clicked shut, he and Google both came out of their stalls.

"In here," Nick said, pointing to the stall the janitor had just cleaned. He and Google rushed into it. They squatted on the toilet seat facing each other, with their backs leaning against the walls and their hands on each other's shoulders for balance. They were in that position when the janitor returned a few minutes later, and they stayed in it, fear etched on their faces, until the janitor dragged his creaky bucket out into the hallway.

"Holy shit," Google whispered, breathing a huge sigh of relief. "I thought I was going to have a heart attack." They unfolded themselves and stepped out of the stall.

"You still want to do this?" Nick asked. Google nodded. Nick opened the washroom door and poked his head out. The hall was deserted. He motioned to Google, and they tiptoed down the corridor, stopping where it intersected the hallway to the main office. Nick peeked around the corner. "We're good," he whispered. They ran to the main office and stepped inside. They crawled toward McAndrew's office, staying well below the windows that overlooked the hallway. A dolly leaned against the wall outside McAndrew's office.

Google opened the door and, giving Nick a thumbs-up, peeled off the piece of tape that had prevented the door from locking and put it in his pocket. The trick had worked, just like it did in the movies.

Google had put the tape on the doorframe that afternoon when he and Nick went to see McAndrew—supposedly to ask the coach if they could have pre-game meals as a team during the Christmas tournament. They knew he wouldn't go for it but they needed a reason to be there so they could do what they'd just done: break into his office to find out if there was anything on his computer that connected him to Albertson's murder.

"Forget it," was McAndrew's response to the suggestion, as he took some folders out of his filing cabinet and placed them in a cardboard packing box. "It would be way too complicated."

"Told you," Google said to Nick, as if it had been Nick's idea, and started to walk out of the office. When he got to the door he dropped the binder he was carrying, spilling papers all over the floor. He bent down to pick them up.

"We'll organize everything," Nick said to McAndrew, moving to other side of the room to divert the coach's attention away from Google.

"How are we supposed to get from the restaurant to the arena with all our gear? We'd need a dozen cars," McAndrew said, shaking his head as if Nick had just made the dumbest suggestion of all time.

"I hadn't thought of that," Nick said—as if he had just made the dumbest suggestion of all time. Out of the corner of his eye Nick saw Google stand up. It had only taken him a few seconds to put the tape over the locking mechanism.

"Apparently not," McAndrew said dryly. "Anything else?" he asked. Nick shook his head. McAndrew grabbed another cardboard box. As Nick walked out the door, he glanced at the tape on the doorframe. You wouldn't see it unless you knew it was there.

Nick turned on his flashlight. He and Google walked around the stack of cardboard boxes beside McAndrew's desk. Google sat down and turned on the computer.

Nick swept his flashlight across the desk. He stopped at the photo of McAndrew in his Kingston Frontenac uniform. There was another photo beside it that Nick hadn't noticed before. Two boys, around ten or eleven, also in hockey uniforms, posing for the camera. McAndrew and his twin brother, Colin, Nick realized. They looked exactly alike. Nick remembered reading an article about identical twins who had been separated at birth. They said that all their lives they felt as if something was missing and that they didn't feel complete until they found each other. Nick wondered if McAndrew felt like part of him went missing after his brother died.

"Look at this," Google said. It was an email McAndrew sent to Marty Albertson on September 15—the day Colin died, and two days before Albertson was murdered. It was short and to the point.

Just wanted to let you know that Colin died today. Not that I expect you to give a shit.

"Did Albertson answer him?"

"That's what I'm looking for." Google scrolled down McAndrew's inbox. He looked at Nick and shook his head. Then he took a computer disk out of his knapsack.

"What's that?" Nick asked.

"It's an email recovery program. It finds emails after they've been deleted." He put the disk in the computer.

Nick waited as Google ran the recovery program. As it

started to load, there was a noise outside the office. Google quickly turned off the computer. The screen went dark.

Nick and Google ducked down under the desk as a key turned in the lock. The door opened. Light flooded into the room. A cellphone rang.

"Hello." Nick recognized McAndrew's voice. The frightened look on Google's face told him his friend recognized the coach's voice too. "Hey, Chris. How's it going? ... All packed? ... Great. I'll meet you at the baggage carousel ... Bye, Chris. See you tomorrow."

"Need any help, Mr. McAndrew?" The janitor's high-pitched voice came from the direction of the doorway.

"Oh, hi John. Thanks for bringing up the dolly. You can help me load those cartons, if you would." *That explains the phone call to the janitor in the washroom,* Nick said to himself.

Google tapped Nick on the arm. He pointed to the window behind the desk. Nick could see the reflections of McAndrew and the janitor as they walked to the far side of the desk where the cartons were stacked. His heart leaped into his throat. If they could see McAndrew, McAndrew could see them. *That's it,* he thought. *I'm going to be suspended from school and kicked off the team, and Dad is going to kill me.* The two of them shrank as far back as they could.

"Any plans for the holidays?" McAndrew asked, as the janitor loaded the boxes onto the dolly.

"Going to the in-laws in Nelson. My wife comes from a family of seven, so it's always a zoo."

"That's the way Christmas is supposed to be," McAndrew said wistfully. "There's just me and my sister now, so it feels kind of lonely." He stared out the window. He seemed to be looking right at Nick. Nick's heart was beating so hard he thought it was going to explode.

"Want me to take this to your car?"

"That'd be great. Thanks, John." The janitor tilted the dolly back and pushed it out of Nick's line of sight. "I'll get the door for you," McAndrew said.

A few seconds later the room went dark, and the door clicked shut.

Nick and Google both exhaled at the same time. They waited a minute or so to make sure McAndrew wasn't coming back, and then crawled out from under the desk. "I thought I was going to shit my pants," Google whispered as he turned McAndrew's computer back on.

"Me too," said Nick. He'd never been so scared in his life. The two of them looked at the computer screen as the email recovery disk searched through McAndrew's deleted emails. A dialogue box appeared on the screen. NO FILES CONTAINING THE WORD ALBERTSON WERE FOUND.

"Let's see what McAndrew was doing on the day Albertson was killed," Nick suggested. Google opened McAndrew's Outlook program and clicked back to September 17. "Holy shit! Look at that," Nick whispered excitedly, pointing to the entry for 6:30 p.m.

Two words were typed there. *Chris. Hospital.*

"What?" Google asked.

"Chris." Nick pointed at the entry.

"What about him?"

"He's Baldy."

"How do you figure that?" Google asked.

"Don't you get it? Dad arrived at the hospital for the fundraiser at 6:45 on the 17th." He pointed at the entry again. "Chris—Baldy—was there at 6:30 so he could put the paint on Dad's suit."

"Holy shit," Google said.

"Let's see if there's anything else about Chris on the computer," Nick suggested.

Google clicked the cursor on FIND, and typed *Chris* in the box. There was one result: December 22. *Chris. AC161. Arrives Van 4:07.*

"The 22nd. That's tomorrow," Google said. "And McAndrew's picking him up."

"How do you know that?" Nick asked.

"That was Chris on the phone with McAndrew just now. Weren't you listening?"

"I was too busy praying."

"It was Chris. And McAndrew said he'd meet him at the baggage carousel."

"Unreal. Unfreakingreal," Nick said.

"Yeah. Let's get out of here," Google said. He shut down McAndrew's computer. The two of them crept to the door. Nick opened it and poked his head out. The coast was clear. He and Google walked out of the room. As Nick pulled the door closed, Google stuck his foot between the door and the frame.

"What are you doing?" Nick whispered. Google didn't answer. He walked over to McAndrew's computer, and opened the disk tray. He took out his email recovery program disk and put it in his knapsack.

"You the man," Nick whispered.

CHAPTER THIRTY-THREE

Google pulled up in front of the domestic terminal at Vancouver International Airport. It was just before three o'clock. AC flight 161 wasn't due for another hour, but they wanted to be sure they were in position before McAndrew arrived.

Nick looked at Google. "Let's do it," he said. They both knew the plan. They'd gone over it a hundred times. They jabbed fists, then Nick got out of the car and watched Google drive off. Google would wait at the gas station on the road leading to the airport and text Nick when he saw McAndrew drive by in his red Honda Element. Meanwhile, Nick would go inside and wait for Baldy, aka Chris, to arrive.

Nick entered the terminal. The flight monitor showed AC 161 arriving at Gate 3 at 4:07 p.m. Right on schedule. He went to the baggage claim area and looked around for a spot where he could be out of sight but still see the passengers arriving. The jewelry stand on the other side of the walkway looked to be perfect. After he checked it out he walked to the Tim Horton's and waited for Google to contact him. He bought a coffee and sat down at the table. It was 3:15. At 3:42 his cellphone beeped. Nick flipped it open. It was a text from Google: He's on his way.

OK, Nick texted back. He took his place at the jewelry stand. At 4:05, McAndrew came up the ramp from the street level. He was carrying a bouquet of flowers. *That's strange,* Nick thought. He texted Google. He's here.

I'm waiting outside, Google texted back.

McAndrew walked over to the baggage carousel for AC 161. A few minutes later the passengers began to file in and gather around the carousel. Nick saw one bald man, but he didn't limp. A short while later, McAndrew waved in the direction of the arriving passengers. An attractive redheaded woman walked up to McAndrew. The two of them hugged.

"What the … ?" Nick muttered to himself. McAndrew and the woman chatted as they stood by the carousel, waiting for the baggage to arrive. A few minutes later, bags started tumbling down the chute. A couple of minutes after that the redhead pointed to a brown suitcase. McAndrew hoisted it off the carousel and the two of them walked away from the baggage area, talking a mile a minute. Nick texted Google. leaving now.

He followed McAndrew and the woman as they walked down the ramp toward the parking area, keeping well back. He felt hopelessly confused. McAndrew wasn't surprised when the woman arrived. He was expecting her. Nick didn't know what to make of that. And McAndrew didn't give her the flowers. He didn't know what to make of that either.

He watched McAndrew and the woman enter the parking garage. A few seconds later Google pulled up. Nick got in the car.

"I don't understand," Google said after Nick brought him up to speed.

"Neither do I." They drove out of the terminal, turned right on a service road, backed into a parking spot and waited for McAndrew's Honda.

"Maybe Baldy couldn't make it and sent the woman instead?" Google suggested.

"Beats me," Nick had no idea what was going on. The only thing he knew for sure was that unless Baldy was wearing a wig and had grown a pair of tits, he wasn't on AC flight 161.

"Here he comes," Google said, as McAndrew's red Honda came into view. Google waited for it to pass, then pulled onto the road and followed it.

Twenty minutes later, Nick was more confused than ever. He and Google were parked on the side of a lane in Mountain View Cemetery, watching McAndrew and the redhead walk across a grassy field dotted with tombstones. They stopped in front of a marble slab under a large oak tree. For a moment Nick had the crazy thought that Marty Albertson was buried there, and that McAndrew and the woman were on some kind of weird trip. Then he remembered that Albertson was buried in Kingston.

McAndrew put the bouquet of flowers on the grave. The woman reached out and took McAndrew's hand. They stood there for a few minutes, then turned and walked back to their car.

"What should we do?" Google asked.

"Follow them," Nick said. "The grave isn't going anywhere."

Google switched on the ignition and pulled out behind McAndrew. He and Nick swapped theories as they followed the Honda Element back to McAndrew's apartment in West Vancouver, but nothing they came up with made any sense. Google turned to Nick after McAndrew and the woman disappeared into the building.

"Back to the cemetery?" he asked. Nick nodded.

It was dark by the time they got back to the cemetery, but it was a clear night, and, using the oak tree as a reference point, they had no trouble finding the grave McAndrew had visited.

Nick shone his flashlight on the tombstone. *Margaret Alice McAndrew*. He swept the flashlight along the rest of the inscription. *Wife of the late Edward Ernest McAndrew. Beloved Mother of Colin, Jack, and Christine.* "It's his mother's grave," Nick said. "Look at this," he said, focusing the flashlight on the last name on the inscription. *Christine.*

"Christine," Google read.

"Christine. Chris," Nick prompted.

"Oh my God. She's his sister."

Suddenly the entry in McAndrew's agenda didn't seem so ominous. In fact, it didn't seem ominous at all. McAndrew and his sister Christine went to the hospital to visit their mother on September 17, the day Albertson was killed. Their mother died twelve days later.

Jack McAndrew had nothing to do with the murder of Marty Albertson.

As far as his dad's case was concerned, he was back at square one. Nick could feel a familiar depression settling over him. By the time Google dropped him off at Al and Helen's, he was back in "the room."

CHAPTER THIRTY-FOUR

Helen brought the turkey in and set it in front of Al's place at the head of the table. Then she sat down at the other end.

"Look at the size of that thing," their youngest son, Jesse, said.

"Twenty-eight pounds," Helen said.

"Where did you get it?" asked Jesse's wife, Elaine.

"At an organic farm in Chilliwack."

"Where else?" said Al.

"Probably had a better diet than 75 per cent of the people on the planet," said Neil, Al and Helen's middle son.

"Probably lived better than 75 per cent of the people on the planet," said Leo, their eldest son.

"Probably could feed 75 per cent of the people on the planet with what it cost," said Al. Everybody laughed.

"I'm glad everybody's having fun," Helen said. "Even if it is at my expense."

"You mean at my expense," said Al. They all laughed again. "It looks delicious, honey," he said, giving Helen an affectionate smile. He stood up. "Merry Christmas," he said, raising his glass. The others followed suit. "To family and friends, present and absent." Al caught Nick's eye and raised his glass in his direction.

"To family and friends," the others said, clinking

glasses. Then they sat down and bowed their heads as Helen said grace.

"God grant us the serenity to accept the things we cannot change, the courage to change the things we can, and the wisdom to know the difference."

"Amen."

Nick repeated the grace to himself as the plates of food were passed around the table. *God grant us the serenity to accept the things we cannot change, the courage to change the things we can, and the wisdom to know the difference.* He knew the words by heart, but he'd never really paid attention to them before. *God grant us the serenity to accept the things we cannot change,* he repeated. That's what his dad was doing, and that's what he had to do too.

"When does the tournament start?" Jesse asked.

"Day after tomorrow," Nick said.

"How are your chances?"

"Pretty good."

"You don't have a chance," Sean said. "Hollyburn hasn't lost a game all year."

"We're ready for them. They're on the other side of the draw. If all goes well, we'll play them in the final." The Lightning had reeled off three straight victories since their win over Surrey, bringing their record to 10–6–1. That was only good enough for fourth place in the overall standings, but next to Hollyburn, they were the hottest team in the league.

"They're going to kick your ass," Sean said.

"Watch your language, Sean," his mother said in a stern voice.

Sean waited a few seconds, then leaned toward Nick. "They're going to kick your ass," he whispered.

After dinner they went into the living room to open presents. Nick had bought a video game for Sean and a gift certificate to Shoppers Drug Mart for Alicia. He gave Helen a pair of earrings he bought in a store on Granville Island that Sherry had taken him to once. Al got a leather wallet.

"These are beautiful, Nick," Helen said, as she tried on the earrings. She gave him a big hug, genuinely touched by the gift.

"Look at this," Al said, holding up the wallet so everybody could see.

"I hope there's enough room in it for all your do-re-mi," Nick said. Everybody laughed.

Al and Helen gave Nick an NHL video game. Neil and his wife, Denise, gave him a gift certificate to HMV. So did Jesse and Elaine. Leo gave him four movie passes to Cineplex.

Helen waited until everybody had gone home before she handed him the present from his father. It was a tiny box, about the size of the one Helen's earrings came in. When Nick opened the box, he just about fell over. Inside was a Honda car key.

"It's out front," Al said.

Nick ran outside. A brand new Honda Civic was parked in the driveway. Nick couldn't believe it.

"Take it for a spin," Al suggested.

Nick opened the door and got in. There was an envelope from his dad taped to the steering wheel. Nick opened it. He was expecting a long, heartfelt letter full of life lessons but there was just a card. "Merry Christmas. Read the manual. Love, Dad."

CHAPTER THIRTY-FIVE

Nick grabbed his car keys and walked into Al's office. Al was on the speakerphone. He hoped it was going to be a short conversation. He didn't want to miss a minute of the visit with his father. The Lightning had won the first two games of the tournament and tomorrow they were playing Hollyburn for the championship. He couldn't wait to tell his dad all about it.

The man Al was talking to spoke English with a heavy French accent. "We got tree feet of snow and more on de way," he said.

"Three feet!" Al said, feigning excitement as he rolled his eyes at Nick. "A real Canadian winter. That's the one thing I miss out here in Vancouver, Jean-Guy."

"Hokay," Jean-Guy said. "I meet you tonight at de airport." Nick was going to drop Al off at the airport on his way back from the prison.

"No need to do that," Al said. "I can stay at a motel."

"You stay with us," Jean-Guy insisted.

"Well, thanks. I'd love to. I look forward to meeting you and Claudette."

"See you den."

Al pushed a button on the speakerphone, ending the call. "Chicoutimi. Any idea where that is?"

Nick shook his head. "No, but I've heard of it. That's where Georges Vezina came from."

"The Vezina Trophy?" Al asked. Nick nodded. The Vezina Trophy was the award given to the best goalie in the NHL.

"They called him the Chicoutimi Cucumber because he was cool as a cucumber." Nick had read that in a book his mom gave him for Christmas one year. It was full of weird facts about the game. He hadn't seen the book in a while. It must have been lost in the move.

"I didn't know that," Al said. "All I know is that I gotta go there and persuade Jean-Guy and Claudette Hébert that their son François should sign with me."

"He's a great player," Nick said. François Hébert was one of the best players in the Quebec Hockey League.

"Which is why he needs me to represent him," Al said, winking at Nick to show that he was joking. Except he wasn't joking. Nobody had a higher opinion of Al than Al. "We got tree feet of snow and more on de way," he said, doing a perfect imitation of Jean-Guy's accented English. "Chicoutimi. Jesus Christ, what I won't do for the game of hockey." He looked at his watch. "We should get going," he said.

Nick and Al stood up as his dad walked toward their table in the visiting room. Nick could see that his father had been hitting the weights. The veins in his forearms were bulging.

"Merry Christmas," his dad said with a big smile.

"Merry Christmas," they answered back.

His dad hugged Al. "Thanks for coming today. I know how busy you are," he said.

"Don't mention it." Al answered. "You two go on outside. I'm sure you have a lot to talk about."

"So," his dad said. "A little girl is at the cemetery with

her mother, visiting her grandmother's grave. On the way out, the girl stops in front of a tombstone and says, "Mommy, do they ever bury two people in the same grave?" "Of course not," she says. "What makes you think that?" The girl points to the tombstone in front of her. "This one says 'here lies an agent *and* an honest man.'" Nick's dad started laughing.

Al turned to Nick. "Your dad's a funny guy," he said.

"Thanks for the car, Dad," Nick said after they entered the bullpen. "It's the best Christmas present ever."

His dad smiled. "I remember when I got my first car," he said. "It was the day I signed with the Canucks. As soon as we walked out of the office, I told Al to take me to the car dealership. An hour later, I drove off the lot with a red Pontiac Firebird. Went straight up to Whistler where a couple of my buddies were hanging out. That night I met your mom at the Longhorn and convinced her to go for a ride with me. When we got to Pemberton, she asked me if I was planning to kidnap her." Nick's dad stared off into space, lost in his memories. After a few moments he came back. "Make sure you stick to the service schedule with the car, or the warranty won't be any good."

"I will."

"You have to take it in at six months or six thousand miles. Whichever comes first."

"I know. I read the manual."

"Are you guys ready for Hollyburn?"

"We're pumped."

They spent the rest of their time talking about hockey. It was a good visit, the best one ever. Even though they were surrounded by the same brick wall and observed by the same prison guards, Nick was able to forget where they were—until they were back in the visiting room and it was time to say goodbye.

"Bye, dad," Nick said. Al was waiting at the door. A wave of sadness washed over him. His father hugged him.

"You know," his dad said. "I remember the day you were born, when your mother handed you to me for the first time. I was only a few years older than you are now. I held you in my arms and I felt like I had been given a huge responsibility. I didn't know if I was up to it. I guess it's something every father worries about. I look at you now, standing in front of me, and I don't see a boy anymore. I see a fine young man who's already been through more than most people twice his age have to deal with, and I realize I must have done something right. I am so proud of you."

"Thanks, Dad."

"No man could have a finer son. I love you, Nick."

"I love you too, Dad."

"Drive carefully. They're calling for rain." His father gave him another hug, then turned and walked away. He gave Nick a final wave before disappearing through the door that led back to the cells. His father was proud of him. Well, he was proud of his father too.

CHAPTER THIRTY-SIX

Ten ... nine ... eight ... Nick and the rest of the players on the bench enthusiastically banged their hockey sticks on the boards as the seconds ticked away. Three ... two ... one. The buzzer sounded. Final score: West Vancouver Lightning 5. Hollyburn Hawks 2.

Nick jumped over the boards and leaped on the pile of players celebrating the team's championship victory in the Christmas tournament. A few minutes later they untangled themselves and lined up at center ice for the awards ceremony.

The entire team erupted in cheers when the convener announced that Kenny Lipton was the tournament's most valuable player. There were more cheers when he announced that Nick and Biggie made the first all-star team and Ivan made the second team.

The celebration continued in the locker room. Everybody was shaking pop cans and spraying them at each other. It wasn't champagne but it would have to do.

The players walked around the locker room, taking pictures of each other with their cellphones. Nick went up to Lipton. "Congratulations on the MVP, Kenny. You deserved it."

"It could have been you, man," Lipton said. "You played great. We all did." Everybody had played well, but Lipton was unstoppable. He scored seven goals in three games and was a threat every time he stepped onto the ice.

Red came over and joined them. "Way to go, dude," he said, jabbing fists with Lipton.

"Let me get a picture of you two," Nick said. Lipton and Red put their arms around each other's shoulders. "Say cheese." He snapped the picture and then gave the phone to Red. "Take one of us," he said, standing beside Kenny.

Red pointed the cellphone at them. "Say boobies," he said.

Across the room, McAndrew and Ivan were talking with Dave Phillips, the head coach of the UBC Thunderbirds. He was an older man with short grey hair. Ivan shook Phillips' hand and walked away. McAndrew caught Nick's eye and motioned for him to come over.

"Congratulations," Phillips said after McAndrew introduced Nick to him. "Nice win."

"Thanks."

"Jack tells me you're thinking of coming to UBC next year."

"If I get in."

"Nick's being modest," McAndrew said. "He had a 77 per cent average last term."

"Terrific," Phillips said. "Coach McAndrew has been singing your praises to me. After seeing you play, I can see why. We could certainly use you on our team."

"Thanks," said Nick.

"Nick is one of the finest young men I've ever coached. On and off the ice." McAndrew said. "Same goes for Ivan. I hope you haven't given out all your scholarships yet," he added with a smile.

"We should be able to come up with something," Phillips said. "I'll talk to the registrar and see if we can get them moving on early admission." He turned to Nick.

"Then we'll sit down and see what we can do for you."

"That's fantastic," Nick said.

"I gotta run," Phillips said to McAndrew. He turned to Nick and shook his hand. "Nice meeting you Nick. I'll be in touch."

"UBC would be a good fit for you," McAndrew said after Phillips walked away. "Dave's a good man. He knows the game, and he knows how to treat his players."

"Thank you for putting in a good word for me, Coach," Nick said.

"It was my pleasure. I meant what I said about you. I have to admit that I was nervous about putting you back on the team, but it was the smartest decision I ever made."

I wonder if he'd feel the same way if he knew that I had suspected him of killing Marty Albertson, Nick thought.

"It would be cool if we both ended up at UBC," Nick said to Ivan, "but you might still get an offer from the States."

"If it happens, it happens, but I'm not holding my breath. I'm not going to some shitty school just 'cause it's south of the border." Like Nick, Ivan had always dreamed of getting a scholarship to an American university, but at 5'8" and 155 pounds, he knew he was unlikely to attract the attention of a big-time hockey program. "It's not like I'm going to make my living playing hockey. I just hope Phillips comes through with the scholarship."

Red came up to them. "What were you guys talking to Phillips about?" Ivan and Nick exchanged a quick look. Red would be jealous if he knew about the scholarships.

"McAndrew told him we were thinking of going to UBC," Nick said. "He said we should definitely go out for the team."

"Cool," Red said. "I should go there, too. Then we

could keep playing together."

Nick glanced at Ivan. They both knew Red wasn't good enough to play college hockey, even if his marks were high enough for him to be accepted into UBC—which they weren't. "That'd be great," he said.

"See you guys at Biggie's," Red said, jabbing fists with both of them. "Seahawks are gonna kick some ass today." The gang was going to Biggie's to watch Seattle play Green Bay. It was the last game of the regular season and a Seattle victory would give them home field advantage throughout the playoffs.

When Nick was leaving the locker room, he noticed Kenny Lipton and his dad talking to the scout from Michigan, the one who'd been at the Surrey game. Mr. Lipton was yakking away in a loud voice. "We've got letters of interest from a couple of other schools, so you guys better not wait too long."

Sherry's sister Amy came running up to Nick, with one of her friends. "Hi Amy," Nick said with a big smile. He hadn't seen her in almost a year. She was a younger version of Sherry, with the same green eyes and red hair. "You've grown," he said.

"Did you expect me to shrink?" Amy asked. She had Sherry's sense of humor too. "This is my friend Sophie."

"Hi Sophie."

"Hi," Sophie said, giving him a gap-toothed grin.

"What did you think of the game?" Nick asked Amy.

"It was great. You destroyed them."

"Number eleven is really good," Sophie said. Eleven was Lipton's number.

"Yes he is," Nick said. "How's your team doing?" he asked.

"Terrible," Amy said. "We haven't won a game yet."

The scout from Michigan shook hands with Kenny and his father, and then headed for the exit. Mr. Lipton went into the washroom, leaving Kenny by himself.

"Hey, Kenny. Come say hello to a couple of friends of mine," Nick said. Lipton sauntered over. "This is Amy and her friend Sophie. Sophie's a big fan of yours," he said to Lipton.

"Can I have your autograph?" Sophie asked.

"Sure," Lipton said. Sophie handed him her program and a pen. Kenny signed his name. "Here you go," he said.

Lipton's father came out of the washroom. "Let's go, sport," he shouted.

"A bunch of us are going to Biggie's to watch the Seahawks," Nick said to Kenny. "You want to come?"

"I can't," Kenny said. "I've got to do some work around the house. That's how I'm paying my dad back for the windows."

"Let's go. I don't have all day," his father shouted. He turned and walked towards the front door of the arena.

"Can't you ask him if you can do it later?"

"You have to be kidding." He glanced in his father's direction. "You know the deal, sport," he said, mimicking his dad. "See you on Tuesday. Bye Amy. Bye Sophie. Nice meeting you."

Kenny trudged after his father. Nick felt sorry for him. The guy was the MVP in one of the biggest tournaments of the year. His team won the championship. One of the best schools in the US was interested in him. He should have been on top of the world. Instead, he looked like he was going to the electric chair. His father had sucked all the joy out of what should have been one of the best days of his life.

CHAPTER THIRTY-SEVEN

"I can't believe school starts in two days," Google said, as he and Nick handed their tickets to a girl in a Cineplex uniform. She tore off the stubs and handed them back.

"Cinema 3," she said, "on the left."

"It sucks," Nick agreed. Aside from practice, he had just kicked back and chilled during the entire week since the tournament. He couldn't remember the last time he'd done that.

"I'm going to get some popcorn," Google said. "Want anything?"

"I'm good."

"Look. Sherry's here," Google said, pointing to the far side of the lobby. Sherry was standing by herself near the washroom.

Bet she's waiting for Joe College, Nick thought. "I'll go inside and get a couple of seats," he said. The last thing he felt like doing was making small talk with Sherry and her boyfriend. Google nodded and joined the lineup at the concession stand. Nick headed for the theatre, feeling like a total wuss. *Be a man,* he said to himself. He turned around and walked over to Sherry.

"Hey," he said.

"Hi, Nick." She gave him a warm smile.

"How were your holidays?" he asked.

"Too short," she said.

"You got that right," Nick said. "What movie you going to?"

"*Eternal Heart.*"

"I should have guessed," he said. He'd seen the trailer. It was a romance about lovers who die in a car crash. Their souls return to earth in different bodies and they spend the rest of the movie looking for each other.

"How about you?" Sherry asked.

"The new Bond movie."

"I should have guessed," Sherry responded. Nick laughed. They had always argued about what movie to see. She liked drama or romance; he preferred action flicks. They ended up taking turns.

"Hey," Google said to Sherry as he walked up to them. He held out his box of popcorn. "Want some?"

"No thanks," she said. "Amy told me you won the Christmas tournament."

"Yeah," Nick said. "We played really well."

"Nick was great. He made the first all-star team," Google said.

"Congratulations," Sherry said.

Nick shrugged. "We won. That's all that matters," he said. The words sounded fake, mostly because they were. Making the tournament all-star team was one of the highlights of his hockey career. He sounded like a player being interviewed on TV, where it was considered bad form to talk about your own achievements.

Sherry picked up on it right away. "Now you're supposed to say that there's no *i* in team," she joked. Nick smiled. He could never put anything past her. Vanessa came out of the woman's washroom and walked up to them.

"Hi, guys," she said with a smile. She turned to Sherry.

"We better get going."

"See you at school," Sherry said. Nick watched them as they walked away. He wondered why Sherry wasn't with her boyfriend on a Saturday night. He warned himself not to jump to any conclusions. He remembered the last time he did that. It hadn't worked out so well.

CHAPTER THIRTY-EIGHT

"Remember, the first draft of your essay is due next Monday," Putnam said at the end of the class. "You've had three weeks to do it, so don't bother asking for an extension. Make sure you include a bibliography of at least three additional sources that you'll be using in your essay."

"How much is it worth?" Emma asked.

"How much is it worth?" Donny Keagan echoed in a disdainful voice. He looked at Fred Feldman, expecting a laugh.

"Grow up, Keagan," Fred said. He smiled at Emma. She smiled back at him.

Putnam ignored the bickering. "It's worth ten per cent of your grade," he answered.

Nick stopped at Sherry's desk on his way out of the classroom. "How's it going?"

"Pretty good," she said. She zipped up her knapsack and stood up. CONFORM. EVERYBODY'S DOING IT. was printed on her white T-shirt. They walked out of the room together. He and Sherry hadn't had much to do with each other in the three weeks since school started—just the occasional conversation between classes—but Nick no longer felt the heartbreaking desire that had made just seeing her so painful over the past few months. He still wanted to be back with her, of course, but it wasn't as if his whole life depended on it. It was a relief to be able to relax and be himself with her.

"Have you decided where you're going next year?" Nick asked.

"I'm leaning toward Emily Carr."

"I thought you wanted to go to the art school in Toronto."

"I've pretty much ruled that out. I'd miss the ocean and the mountains too much." Nick wondered if that was all she'd miss. "Besides, the skiing in Ontario sucks."

"I know," Nick said. "I went to Blue Mountain a couple of years ago when I was visiting my uncle and aunt. They have no right to call it a mountain, not when it takes less than a minute to get down a run."

Sherry laughed. "What are you doing next year?" she asked.

"I'm going to UBC. I got a hockey scholarship." The letter from Coach Phillips had arrived on Friday. He had taken it to the prison with him on Saturday. His dad had been as excited as Nick thought he'd be.

"That's fantastic!"

"You'll have to come to a game."

"It's not *that* fantastic," she replied. Nick laughed. Nobody made him laugh like she did. "How's your dad doing?" she asked.

"He's pretty good. He's going to be transferred to a prison in Mission." The transfer had been approved, but it was going to take a couple of months for the paperwork to be processed. "Instead of being in a cell, he'll be living apartment-style and doing his own cooking. He's really looking forward to it."

"How about you?"

"It's important to him, so it's important to me. But it's still a prison."

Sherry nodded sympathetically. "Say hi for me the next time you speak to him."

"I will."

"I'd like to visit him once he gets transferred. Do you think that would be okay?"

"He'd love it."

"I gotta run," Sherry said, looking at her watch. "I start work at four."

"Practice doesn't start until four-thirty. I'll give you a lift."

"That would be great. Thanks."

"I love this song," Sherry said, as *Yesterday* came on the car radio.

"Still a big Beatles fan?" Nick said.

"Greatest band ever." She turned up the volume. They were sitting in the parking lot at Park Royal. The sun streamed through the windshield, lighting up her face. *She's so beautiful,* Nick thought for the zillionth time. But for the first time in a long time, he could look at her without feeling like he was being kicked in the stomach. Maybe they could be friends after all.

They listened to the rest of the song in silence. That was something else he always liked about Sherry. If she didn't have anything to say, she didn't feel like she had to talk just to fill in the space the way a lot of other people did. He hoped Joe College knew how lucky he was. The car was warm from the sun. Nick leaned back and let the music wash over him.

"I've got to tell you something," Sherry said when the song came to an end. The serious look on her face made him imagine the worst. *Joe College and I are getting married.* He instantly dismissed the thought. *I've seen too many movies,* he said to himself.

"Michael and I broke up."

It took him a second to put it together. *Michael. So that's his name.* He stared at Sherry, but her face wasn't giving anything away. *Had she ended it, or had he?* Either way it was good news as far as he was concerned. He wasn't sure how to react, other than knowing it probably wouldn't be a good idea to shout "All right!" and give her a high five. "What happened? You two seemed to have a good thing going," he said, thinking back to the scene he'd witnessed at the mall the day he made an ass of himself.

Sherry shrugged. "Appearances can be deceiving," she said. "Michael's a nice guy, but he was always telling me what to do. I didn't feel like I could be myself with him."

That answered Nick's question about who ended it. "When did this happen?" he asked.

"Just before Christmas break."

A month ago. "How come you waited until now to tell me?"

"I didn't want you to get your hopes up. I didn't know if I wanted to start seeing you again."

"Why are you telling me now?" he asked. The answer was obvious, but he wanted to hear her say it.

"Why do you think? Because I want to start seeing you again."

"You do?" he said. He couldn't keep his voice from cracking.

She nodded. "But I want to take things slow." It was his turn to nod. "I need to know that what happened before isn't going to happen again."

"It won't," he promised. "I was messed up. I wasn't myself."

"I know that," she said. "I can see that you've changed.

That's why I want to give us another chance. But I still want to take it slow," she repeated.

Nick knew what that meant. No sex. "I totally understand," he said. "We'll take it as slow as you want," he added. He meant it too. Not that he had much of a choice.

"Great." Sherry looked at her watch. "Shit. I'm late." She leaned across and kissed him on the cheek. She opened the door and got out of the car. They stared at each for a long moment.

"I'll call you tonight," he said. She smiled and then walked away.

"That's it?" he said out loud. He couldn't help feeling let down. Whenever he'd imagined getting back together with Sherry, and he'd imagined it more times than he could count, the scene had always been full of emotion—a long passionate embrace accompanied by tears of joy and mutual declarations of love. He never dreamed it would be like this—an announcement and a kiss on the cheek. Putnam would call that an anti-climax.

Sherry disappeared inside the mall. He stared at the glass doors for a while. The feeling of disappointment began to fade away as the reality sunk in. He and Sherry were back together again! So what if there were no fireworks. There was plenty of time for that. He wondered what length of time Sherry had in mind when she said she wanted to "take it slow." *I guess I'll find out,* he said to himself. He started the car and put it in reverse. As he was backing out of the parking spot, his cellphone rang. He looked at the display. It was Kenny Lipton.

"Hey Kenny. How's it going?"

"Can you meet me at Mike's before practice?"

"Sure. What's up?"

"I'll tell you when I see you."

Kenny was sitting in a booth when Nick arrived. "Thanks for coming," he said.

"What's going on?" Nick asked. "You sounded pretty serious on the phone."

"I'm moving back to Ottawa."

"Ottawa!"

"Yeah. I'm going to go live with my mom. I can't hack it here with my dad anymore. We almost got in a fist fight the other day."

"Holy shit!"

"Yeah."

"When are you leaving?"

"Friday." *This sucks,* Nick thought. *Just when the team has hit its stride.* The Lightning had followed up its victory in the Christmas tournament with four straight wins, moving the team into second place in the league. Hollyburn had first place all locked up, but with Lipton leading the way—the man was a human scoring machine—the team was confident that they could beat them come playoff time.

"I didn't know your parents were separated."

"Yeah. Mom left him a couple of years ago."

"Why didn't you stay in Ottawa with her?"

"I felt I owed it to my dad to come with him when he was transferred out here. Ever since I was a kid, he was the one who got up early and drove me to practice. In all the years I played, he never missed a game. It would have killed him not to see me play hockey."

"Have you told McAndrew?" Nick asked.

"Yeah. He said he could find me somewhere else to live if I wanted to stay for the rest of the year. I thought about it, but it would be way too complicated."

"What did your dad say when you told him?"

"'Suit yourself, sport,'" Kenny said, imitating his father. "'But if you go out that door, you aren't coming back in.' He wasn't always like this, you know," he added. "He took it real hard when my mom left."

That doesn't give him the right to treat you like a piece of dirt, Nick thought. "Are you going play in Ottawa?"

"I made some calls. A couple of teams are interested."

"We're really going to miss you, Kenny."

"It goes both ways. I feel bad about leaving you guys like this."

"You've gotta do what's right for you," Nick said.

"You better get going or you'll be late for practice," Kenny said. They stood up and walked out of the diner. Kenny stuck out his hand. Nick took it. "Good luck with the rest of the season. I'll be pulling for you guys."

Nick nodded. He watched Kenny walk away. *Just goes to show,* he thought, *you should never be too quick to judge people.* If somebody had told him two months ago that Kenny Lipton had more guts than anybody he knew—and that he'd be sad to say goodbye to him—Nick would have said he was out of his mind.

CHAPTER THIRTY-NINE

Nick stood at his own blue line and took a couple of deep breaths. The score was tied after sixty minutes of regulation hockey. Neither team had scored in ten minutes of overtime. The shootout was all-even at two goals apiece. It was up to him. If he scored, the Lightning would win the championship. The puck sat at center ice. Nick moved toward it, but something didn't feel right. When he looked down he saw he was wearing his winter boots instead of his skates. He wondered how that could have happened, but there was no time to think about it. He cradled the puck with his stick and slowly jogged toward the net. The goalie came out of the crease, cutting off the angle. Nick knew he wouldn't be able to deke him out in his winter boots, so he faked a shot to the glove side and then slapped a low screamer to the stick side. It hit the inside of the post and caromed into the net.

Nick turned and ran back toward his teammates. Sherry was the first one out on the ice. She jumped into his arms. Suddenly they were in bed, naked under the sheets. Someone was knocking on the door. He and Sherry looked at each other, panic-stricken. The knocking continued.

Nick woke up in a sweat. He was in his own bed. Alone.

"Your dad's on the phone," Helen called out. "You can take it in Al's office."

"I'm coming," he shouted. He got of bed and put on his jeans. He and Sherry had been together for three weeks now but his dreams were the only place where they were having sex. She had been serious when she said she wanted to take things slow.

Nick walked into Al's office and picked up the phone. "Hi Dad."

"Listen, Nick. I've got some bad news." The first thing Nick thought of was that the transfer had been denied. "Grandpa died last night."

"Oh, no," Nick said.

"Yeah," his father said in a sad voice.

"I'm sorry, Dad."

"He died in his sleep. At least he didn't suffer."

"That's good."

"I don't have time to talk right now. I've got to make some calls. The funeral's on Sunday. They're giving me a pass. We'll fly to Saskatoon Sunday morning, go to the funeral, and come back the same night. I'll call you later when I've made all the arrangements, all right?"

"Okay, Dad."

Nick hung up. He didn't know his grandfather very well. He used to come to Vancouver for a week every summer when Nick was younger, but all Nick remembered was that he spent most of his time smoking on the porch. The visits stopped when Nick was around ten, and his grandfather moved into a nursing home in Saskatoon. He and his dad would go and see him once a year. Nick's dad wanted to move him to Vancouver but he wouldn't come. He'd lived in Saskatoon his whole life, and the few friends he had left still lived there.

The last time Nick had seen his grandfather was the summer before his dad went to jail. The nursing home was depressing. A group of residents sat in front of the TV, watching a soap opera. Most of them wore their bathrobes. One old guy lay asleep in a wheelchair by the window, his mouth open. Nick tried not to stare. It was hard to believe that they had all once been his age. And even harder to believe that one day he would be theirs. His grandfather was in his room. He was hooked up to an oxygen tank, but that didn't stop him from smoking. "Let's go get some fresh air," he said in his raspy voice, when Nick and his dad arrived.

As soon as they were outside, his grandfather lit up. "Promise me you'll never start smoking, Nicky," he croaked. He coughed up a giant piece of phlegm and spit it out on the grass. It lay there like a clam. Nick had looked at his grandfather, sitting in his wheelchair with tubes coming out of his nose, hacking his guts out. "I promise, Grandpa," he said.

Even though he didn't have much of a relationship with his grandfather, Nick felt sad as he went back to his room. They must have done stuff together when he came to Vancouver to visit, but Nick couldn't summon up a single memory. All he could remember was an old man in a wheelchair with a raspy voice and a smoker's cough.

CHAPTER FORTY

Pete took his dad's handcuffs off ten minutes after the plane took off from Saskatoon on the return flight home from the funeral. "Come sit beside your father," he said to Nick, who was seated across the aisle beside a second prison guard named Roland.

"Thanks Pete," Nick's father said gratefully. A little too gratefully for Nick's taste, although he knew Pete was doing them a favor. The two of them hadn't had a moment alone since they'd left Vancouver International Airport early that morning. As soon as they arrived in Saskatoon, they drove straight to the funeral parlor. After the service they all drove out to the cemetery for the burial. Then they drove directly to the airport to catch the flight to Vancouver.

Nick took the seat beside his father. His dad put his arm across Nick's shoulder and gave him a one-armed hug. "You okay?" he asked.

"I thought there'd be more people at the funeral," he said. Aside from Nick and his dad and the two guards, the only people at the service were two old friends of his grandfather, and Nick's Aunt Alison, his father's older sister, who had flown in from Kansas City. Alison came to the airport with them so that they would have a chance to talk, but Alison and Nick's dad had never been very close. The last time they'd seen each other was when Nick's mom died. With the two guards listening to every word, the conversation was awkward, to say the least. Everybody was relieved when it was time to board the flight.

"Most of Grandpa's friends are dead," his dad explained. He stared out the window for a few moments, and then turned back to Nick. "It's funny, the things you remember," he said. "I remember one time when I was six or seven. I was playing outside with a rope, whipping it around an oak tree we had in the backyard. I must have hit a beehive. All of a sudden, hundreds of angry bees started attacking me. My father heard me screaming and came rushing out of the house. He wrapped me up in his arms to protect me, and carried me into the house. He got stung so often his face was swollen for days." He stared off into the distance, lost in his thoughts.

"I think he knew his time had come. The last time we spoke, a couple of weeks ago, he told me that he loved me. He never said that before. It was like he was determined to say it before it was too late. I knew he loved me, but it still felt good to hear him say it." Nick's dad paused for a moment.

"Did he come to your games when you were a kid?"

"Rarely. We usually played on Saturdays, and he had to be at the hardware store."

"He could have come if he'd really wanted to," Nick said.

"That's true," his father agreed.

"Did it bother you?" Nick asked.

"Not at the time. That was just the way it was. I knew he cared about me. And I think he saw that I was getting along okay, so in his mind it wasn't necessary. He was a good man, kind and gentle, but he was a stranger. I never told him anything about my life, at least not about my inner life, about how I felt. We didn't have the same kind of relationship you and I do. I know you don't tell me everything—it would be pretty weird if you did." His dad smiled at him. "But I know you in a way my father never knew me. I don't think he ever realized what *he* was missing out on. Fatherhood has been one of the great joys of my life. It's definitely the most rewarding thing I've ever done."

"More than winning the Stanley Cup?"

"Not even close."

A half-hour later they were flying over the Rockies. Nick looked out the window. Snow-capped mountains stretched out as the far as the eye could see. He wished they could stay on the airplane forever.

"Pretty spectacular, isn't it?" his dad said. "When's your next game?"

"Tomorrow. Against Aldergrove," Nick said. "It's going to be a tough one. They've been on a roll." *Unlike us*, he thought. The team had lost its first two games after Kenny Lipton left the team, including an 8-2 shellacking at Hollyburn last Monday. It wasn't just the fact that they'd lost, that bothered Nick so much. It was the way they lost: everybody blaming everybody else; nobody taking responsibility for the way they were playing. Ivan called a team meeting after the game, without the coaches, to clear the air. The team had responded by routing a solid Cloverdale team 6-0. That was a positive sign, but they needed a good showing against Aldergrove to convince themselves they were back on track.

"Do you want to see some photos from the Christmas tournament?" Nick asked.

"You bet."

Nick flipped open his cellphone and handed it to his

dad. He scrolled through the photographs, asking Nick to identifying the players he didn't recognize. "I'd like a print of this one," his dad said when he got to a photo of Nick with his all-star trophy. "A big eight by ten print."

"Would you like something to drink," the flight attendant asked.

"I'll have a Coke, please," Nick said.

She poured some Coke into a plastic glass and handed it to Nick. "Anything for you, sir?" she asked. Nick's father didn't answer. Nick turned and looked at him. He was staring at the cellphone, looking like he'd seen a ghost. "Care for anything to drink, sir?" the attendant repeated.

"Nothing," his dad said, his eyes riveted on the phone. Nick looked at the screen. It was the photo of the bald guy he'd taken at the Vancouver Giants game a couple of months earlier: the guy with no eyebrows. Nick had forgotten all about him.

"That's him," his dad said, a look of disbelief on his face. "That's the man I saw at the hospital, the man who put the paint on my jacket. Where did you take this?"

"At a Giants game a couple of months ago," Nick said. "Are you sure it's him?"

"It's him. It's definitely him," he said, still looking at the photo. "No eyebrows. That's what I couldn't remember. All I could remember was that bald head and the way he limped away." He looked at Nick. His face was flushed with excitement. "Who is he? Did you follow him? Do you know where he lives?"

Nick shook his head. "I don't know anything about him. He was going up the escalator when we were going down. I watched him get off to see if he limped but he got lost in the crowd before I could see anything. Google and I went to a bunch of Giants games after that, but we never saw him again."

"Unbelievable. Unbelievable," his dad said, still staring at the picture. Nick couldn't believe it either. His dad looked out the window, lost in thought. After a few seconds he turned back to Nick. "Okay," he said. "Here's what we're going to do."

CHAPTER FORTY-ONE

Nick walked through the lobby of the gleaming skyscraper on West Hastings and rode the elevator up to the 25th floor. He turned left toward the offices of Cuthbert Investigations Inc., the detective agency his father had hired after his arrest. Nick didn't expect Paul Cuthbert to be a slick-looking, fast-talking, chain-smoking character sitting in a dusty office like Jack Nicholson in *Chinatown*—one of his dad's best movie night choices ever—but he was more than a little surprised to find himself in a swanky reception area with matching leather couches, shaking hands with a tall, pot-bellied man who didn't look as though he could fight his way out of a paper bag.

But Nick warmed up to Cuthbert as soon as he said that he believed Nick's dad was innocent. "The whole case made no sense to me, but what really convinced me was his story about a bald man with a limp, putting paint on his jacket. Nobody could make up something like that."

Cuthbert led Nick into his corner office. "Take a seat," he said, pointing to the armchair in front of his desk. Cuthbert opened his dad's file and took out an eight by ten blow-up of the picture of Baldy that Nick had emailed to him. "We could have used this at the trial," he said.

No shit, Nick thought.

"Your dad's positive this is the guy?" Cuthbert asked.

"One hundred per cent. Do you think you'll be able to

find him?"

"We'll do our best. You said you saw him at a Vancouver Giants game?" Cuthbert asked. "Tell me exactly what happened."

It didn't take Nick long to fill him in. "What happens now?" he asked when he was finished.

"I work with agencies in every major city in the country. I'll send the picture to them. It looks like we were right about this guy being a hockey fan, so we'll start by checking out the local hockey rinks. Did you speak to your father about putting an ad in the newspapers?"

"I spoke to him last night. He said to go ahead."

Cuthbert had suggested they put an ad with Baldy's photo in newspapers across the country, offering a fifty thousand dollar reward to anybody who gave information that led to their finding him. It meant taking the chance that Baldy would see the ad and disappear into the woodwork, but his dad was willing to risk it.

"Who were the Giants playing the day you saw him?" Cuthbert asked.

"The Kootenay Ice."

"Where are they from?"

"Cranbrook."

"I'll send one of my men there."

"You think he's from Cranbrook?" Nick asked.

Cuthbert shrugged. "You said you didn't see him at any other Giants games. Maybe he's a Kootenay fan."

Nick was impressed. The thought had never occurred to him. "What happens when we find him?" he asked.

"First things first," Cuthbert cautioned. "Let's find him. Then we'll figure out what to do next."

After the meeting with Cuthbert ended, Nick walked to the

parking lot, oblivious of the rain, trying to sort through his emotions. Ever since his dad was convicted Nick had focused on finding Baldy. It was his only goal, and in his mind, finding Baldy put an end to his nightmare. If he found him, his dad was coming home. It was as simple as that.

But it wasn't as simple as that. Having Baldy's picture was huge, the first solid lead they'd had. But it was only the beginning of the journey. Even if they found Baldy, it didn't mean his father would be released.

"Let's not get too excited," his dad warned him when they spoke on the phone the night before. "First we have to find him, then we have to find out who hired him. And I highly doubt he's going to tell us."

"I know," Nick said. But it took hours before he was able to fall asleep. A scene he hadn't allowed himself to imagine for a long time kept forcing its way into his mind's eye. There he was, standing outside the prison as the front doors opened and his father walked out, a free man.

Nick pulled out of the parking lot and headed north on Burrard. His stomach was in knots. In the past month he had finally started to feel more like his old self, as though he'd come out of a long, dark tunnel. It hadn't been easy, but he'd managed to come to terms with his father's imprisonment and get on with his life. Now all those old feelings were stirred up again.

Nick turned left on West Georgia, heading back to Al and Helen's house. It wasn't until he approached the exit for 21st Street that he remembered the Lightning had a game in Aldergrove—in the opposite direction. He looked in the mirror, signaled, and darted into the exit lane. He'd have to boot it if he didn't want to be late for the game.

CHAPTER FORTY-TWO

Nick woke up before his alarm went off. He started his day the same way he had started every day since they'd placed the ad offering a reward for information about Baldy three weeks earlier. First he checked the voice mail for the toll-free number in the ad. There were no messages. Then he turned on his computer and logged into the email account Cuthbert had set up.

A copy of the ad was taped to the wall above Nick's desk. Below the banner that read: HAVE YOU SEEN THIS MAN?—$50,000 REWARD, it showed the photo of Baldy. His approximate height and weight—5'9" and 150 pounds—were written underneath the photo, along with a 1-800 number and an email address.

There was no mention of Baldy's limp. It was Cuthbert's idea to leave that out. "Rewards attract a lot of nutcases," the detective said. "If people know we're looking for somebody with a limp, they'll tell us their guy has one, even if he doesn't. This way we'll be able to weed out the false leads."

There had been a huge response the first week the ad ran, but the numbers had slipped since then, so Nick wasn't surprised that there were no phone messages and only three emails. He opened the first one.

I could hardly believe it when I saw the picture in the paper. That's my cousin Eddie. Eddie Armstrong. I've known him all my life.

A lot of people think he shaved off his eyebrows but he was born without them. He lives on 9th St. in Canmore, Alberta. I don't know the street number, but he spends most of the day in the Tim Horton's around the corner. Please send the reward to Leon Courtemanche, P.O. Box 48, Flin Flon MB R1A 2K5.

When the ad first came out, the email would have sent Nick's hopes soaring. But he had learned to take even the most positive identification with a grain of salt. Cuthbert's idea to hold back the info about Baldy's limp had been a good one. They had received close to a hundred emails so far, and he'd been able to eliminate all the suspects with a follow-up phone call that revealed that none of them limped.

Nick opened the second email.

I saw the picture in the Halifax Herald. The guy you're looking for is Joe Rossiter. He lives in the apartment building on Gerrish Street where my brother Lenny lives. I know you have to check this out, but he's your guy. No doubt about it. If you speak to Lenny, don't tell him about the reward. He'll insist I give him a piece, and I don't see why he should get anything.

Nick smiled at this example of brotherly love, then moved on to the third message.

I know the guy in the photo. He lives right here in Huntsville. He moved here from BC the year before last. I can't remember exactly when. End of September or maybe early October.

Nick's heart started beating faster. Albertson was murdered on September 17. It made sense that Baldy would leave town then. Everybody in Vancouver knew about the bald man with a limp. He would have been crazy to stick around.

Nick went downstairs for breakfast. He knew he shouldn't get too excited about the lead until Cuthbert checked it out, but his heart wasn't listening to his head.

Al was on the phone, as usual. "I spoke to the lawyer, and he said François will get an unconditional discharge … Okay, *au revoir*," he said, butchering the pronunciation. Al hung up. He turned to Nick. "I don't believe it," he said. "The cops caught François Hébert and a teammate smoking pot in the locker room last night after their game. In the locker room!" he said, incredulous. "How dumb is that?"

"Pretty dumb," Nick said.

He remembered the night his dad caught him and Red smoking a joint outside their house. He was in grade 7, so he must have been twelve. His dad didn't say a word to them. He just went back in the house and waited for Nick to come in.

"How often do you smoke pot?" he asked in a calm voice, when Nick finally summoned up the courage to go inside. Nick told him the truth. Once or twice a month. His father didn't get angry like he thought he would. "Marijuana's illegal, and it's bad for your health," he said. "And I think you're foolish to smoke it, especially at your age, when your lungs are still developing. But short of locking you up, I can't keep you from doing it, so I'm not going to waste my breath ordering you to stop. But as long as it's against the law, I don't want it happening on my property."

"Your dad rocks," Ivan had said, when he told him. "My father would have gone ape shit."

His father did rock, Nick thought. He was smart, too. If he had ordered Nick to quit, Nick wouldn't have stopped smoking, he would have stopped talking to his father. His dad had always treated him with respect. That's why Nick felt he could tell him anything.

Not that he didn't have his secrets. There were some things you just didn't talk to your dad about, no matter how cool he was. The things he and Sherry used to do, for instance. Things he had hoped they'd be doing again by now, but weren't.

"Any action on the ad?" Al asked, interrupting his thoughts.

"We got a few responses."

"Anything interesting?"

"Maybe," Nick said. He told Al about the guy who had moved to Ontario from B.C.

"Sounds promising," Al said. "If I was this guy, I wouldn't want to stick around here." He looked at his watch. "Gotta to get going. I'll see you later."

"See you." Nick fixed himself a bowl of cereal and sat down at the counter. He was reaching for the sports section when the phone rang. Nick recognized the number on the call display. It was his father.

"Hi, dad."

"Hey, Nick. How are you doing?"

"Good. Just getting ready to go to school."

"How was the concert?"

"Fantastic. Google said to say thanks." Nick had taken Google to see Cliques and Friques the night before. He told Nick it would be okay with him if he wanted to take Sherry instead, but Nick wouldn't hear of it. He'd already invited Google. He wouldn't be much of a friend if he'd do that—even though he had spent most of the concert wishing Sherry was with him.

"The seats were okay?"

"Are you kidding? We were in the fifth row in the middle section."

"I'm glad you had a good time. You guys ready for the

game?" The Lightning had finished the season with five straight wins, ending up in a tie for second place with Surrey. Tonight was their first playoff game.

"We're ready, but Ridge Meadows is going to give us a game. They beat Hollyburn last week. Only game Hollyburn lost all season."

"Whatever happens, you guys have had a great year."

"It won't mean anything unless we win the championship," Nick said.

"You can't go around thinking the season will be a failure if you don't win the championship."

"What are you saying?" Nick asked. "That we shouldn't care whether we win or lose?"

"Not at all," his dad answered. "It's important to have a goal, and to do everything you can to achieve it. But it's this idea that 'winning isn't everything, it's the only thing,' that I don't agree with. If that's your attitude, you're setting yourself up for a lot of disappointment."

"Come on," Nick argued. "You're not glad you won the Stanley Cup?"

"Of course I am. But I'm tired of hearing everybody say it's all about the ring," he said, referring to the ring team members get for winning a championship. You heard it from players in every sport. The only thing that mattered was getting the ring. Preferably several. "Don't get me wrong," his dad continued. "It was a tremendous thrill to win the Stanley Cup, and it's great to know that my name will be engraved on it forever. But that's not what I remember most about playing. It's the people I played with, the experiences we shared, both good and bad. Life isn't about the goal, Nick. It's about the journey."

Fair enough, Nick thought. But it didn't make winning the championship any less important.

"What else is doing?" his dad asked.

"That's about it," Nick said. He knew his dad wasn't asking about the case. His initial excitement after he identified Baldy had worn off. "I don't want to hear it," he told Nick the last time he visited, when Nick tried to tell him about the latest batch of emails. "I can't get caught up in this. It'll drive me crazy. I need to operate on the assumption that we're not going to find Baldy. If we do find him, you can tell me. Otherwise, we're done talking about it." He looked Nick in the eye. "Understood?" he said in a voice that meant the conversation was over.

Nick understood. He was dying to tell his dad about the latest lead, but he didn't dare bring it up. *Still,* he couldn't help thinking after he hung up, *maybe I'll able to talk to Dad about the case soon. Real soon.*

CHAPTER FORTY-THREE

"Cuthbert left a voice mail for the guy who sent the email," Nick told Google, as they drove to La Fortuna. "He promised he'll call as soon as he hears back."

The detective had been quick to follow up on the three emails they'd received the day before. Cousin Eddie from Flin Flon didn't limp. Neither did J.R. from Halifax. That left the guy who moved to Huntsville from B.C. just after Marty Albertson was killed. Nick was trying not to let his hopes run away with him, but he wasn't doing a very good job.

Biggie, Ivan, and Red were already seated at their table when Nick and Google walked into the restaurant. The Lightning had beaten Ridge Meadows the night before in the first round of the playoffs. Tonight they were playing Surrey in the semi-finals. Hollyburn was facing off against Aldergrove in the other semi-final. The winners would play for the championship tomorrow.

Nick sat down beside Biggie. "What's up?" Biggie asked.

"It's all good," Nick said. He didn't say anything about the case. Except for Google, he had stopped talking about it with the guys. They had all been excited when the ad with Baldy's picture first came out, but after a couple of weeks of nothing but disappointments there didn't seem to be any point talking about it. It just bummed everybody out.

Angelina came out of the kitchen. She called out to Red. "Give me a hand with the drinks, Giovanni."

"What do you guys want?" Red asked.

"I'll have a Coke," Nick said.

"Same here," said the others. Red disappeared into the kitchen.

"Are you sure you don't want a glass of milf?" Google asked Ivan. The table erupted in laughter.

Red came out of the kitchen with a tray of drinks. He passed them out and then sat down.

"I forgot to tell you guys," Nick said. "I got a text from Kenny Lipton. He got the scholarship to Michigan. A full ride."

"That's fantastic," Ivan said.

"Man, if he was still playing with us, Hollyburn wouldn't have a chance," Red said.

"Forget about Hollyburn," Biggie said, "and forget about Kenny Lipton. We have to focus on Surrey."

"No worries," Red said confidently as his mother came out of the kitchen with an armful of plates. "We're gonna wax them."

Red was right. The Lightning trounced Surrey 4–1.

"Congratulations, gentlemen," McAndrew said when he came into the locker room after the game. "You almost looked like a hockey team out there." Nick took a close look at the coach. Was that actually a smile on his face?

"Are you okay, Coach?" Red asked, with mock concern. McAndrew handed out compliments like they were thousand-dollar bills. Everybody laughed.

"We've come a long way since the start of the year. You guys have shown a lot of character," McAndrew said. "Enjoy it for the rest of the day, but we've still got some work to do. Game tomorrow is at seven. Pre-game meeting is at six," he added before limping out of the room.

Nick got to the mall a couple of minutes before nine. Sherry was at the cash register, ringing up a sale. He caught her eye and motioned that he'd wait for her in the hallway. At nine o'clock she came out of the store.

"How was the game?" she asked.

"We won, 4–1."

"Congratulations. Did you score a touchdown?"

"Ha, ha. Very funny."

Sherry shrugged. "It's been a long day. What time is the game tomorrow?"

"Seven. Any way you can get off work?"

"I already took care of it. I knew you guys were going to win, so I switched shifts with Claire." She pulled the grille across the doorway and locked it in place.

"Look at that," Sherry said when they walked into Delaney's. She pointed to a table at the back. Fred Feldman and Emma Jenkins were sitting there, holding hands, staring into each other's eyes as if the rest of the word didn't exist.

Nick looked around for a table. The only one that was free was next to Fred and Emma, who had started to make out. "Let's get out of here," he said. Sherry nodded. "We can go to Starbucks," Nick suggested when they were outside. It was next door to Delaney's.

"We could," Sherry agreed, "or we could go back to my house. My mom's gone to Salt Spring for the weekend to visit Grandma, and Amy's at a sleepover." Nick looked into her eyes. She held his gaze. He leaned down and kissed her. A long lingering kiss that had two years of yearning behind it.

"I missed you so much," Nick said to Sherry afterwards. They were lying in bed on their sides, looking at each other.

"I missed you too."

"I don't want us to ever be apart again," he said. He reached out and stroked her face. She held his hand against her face.

"I love you, Nick Macklin," she said.

"I love you, too."

They lay there silently for a few moments. "I have to pee," Sherry said. She hopped out of bed and walked out of the room. Nick watched her leave. He lay back on the bed. He felt at peace for the first time in a long time.

His cellphone rang. He leaned over, grabbed his jeans off the floor, and took the phone out of one of the pockets.

"Hello."

"It's Bob Cuthbert here, Nick." Nick was instantly alert. "I just spoke to the guy in Huntsville. No luck I'm afraid. The guy who moved there from BC doesn't limp."

"I see," Nick said. He thought he'd be disappointed but he didn't feel anything.

"I know it doesn't look good, Nick," Cuthbert said, "but sooner or later we'll find him. We just have to be patient."

"For sure."

"All right. I'll speak to you later." Cuthbert signed off. Nick closed his cellphone and put it on the bedside table.

"Who was that?" Sherry asked when she came back into the bedroom.

"Cuthbert." He shook his head.

"Oh, Nick," she said. "I'm so sorry."

Nick walked to the window and stared out at the street.

The boys who lived across the road were playing ball hockey in their driveway. Sherry came up beside him. She reached down and took his hand in hers. They stood there for a couple of minutes, not talking, just looking out the window at the two boys. The older boy was in goal. His brother kept firing shot after shot, but he couldn't get one past him.

That's that, Nick thought as a profound feeling of discouragement swept over him. *Dad is never going to get out of jail.* His shoulders sagged, as if all his strength had suddenly deserted him. Sherry squeezed his hand tightly in a gesture of support. Nick could hear his father's voice as clearly as if he was in the room with him. *Winners never quit, and quitters never win.*

"Are you all right?" Sherry asked.

"I am," he said, as he straightened up.

Across the street, the younger boy found the corner of the net with a slapshot. He ran around the driveway, celebrating as if he'd just scored the winning goal in the Stanley Cup.

CHAPTER FORTY-FOUR

Nick looked around the locker room. It was as quiet as a tomb. Everybody was lost in their own thoughts, thinking about the biggest game of their lives. McAndrew came through the door. The room went even quieter. He stood there silently for a few seconds, his eyes moving from player to player.

"This is it, boys," he said. "This is what a final should be. The two best teams in the league squaring off against each other. Talent wise, there's not a lot to choose between us. From here on in, it's all about will. Whoever wants it more is going to walk away with the championship. Look around this room. Look at your teammates. Think about what we've been through this year. Think about how far we've come since the start of the season. Think about how hard you've worked to get to where you are. Not just this year, but ever since you started playing hockey. There's nothing more Charlie and I can do now. It's up to you. The only way we're going to lose is if Hollyburn wants it more than you do. Are you going to let that happen?"

"Hell, no," Red shouted. The rest of the team joined in, pounding their sticks on the floor. "Hell, no. Hell, no." McAndrew smiled in satisfaction, and then limped out of the room.

Ivan stood up and walked to the middle of the room. "Bring it in," he said. Everybody gathered around him.

"We know what we have to do," he said. "Let's get out there and do it."

"One. Two, Three—Lightning!"

The team filed out of the locker room and headed for the ice. Nick and Ivan were the last to leave. Nick couldn't remember ever feeling this nervous before a game. He could see that Ivan was just as tense. "If we played them ten times, they might win nine," he said.

"... But not this game," Ivan continued, with a smile. "Not tonight. Tonight we are the greatest hockey team in the world."

Nick smiled back at Ivan. "Let's do it," he said.

The team answered McAndrew's challenge. They were ready to play the moment the puck was dropped. But so was Hollyburn. It was a tight defensive game from the start. Neither team was able to manufacture a good scoring opportunity, until the Hawks scored on a goalmouth scramble with less than three minutes left in the period to take a 1–0 lead into the locker room.

Nick, Ivan, and Red weren't able to get anything going. Jamie Balfour, the Hollyburn center, shadowed Nick every time he was on the ice, clutching and grabbing in an effort to slow him down. The ref was letting everything go. Nick was growing more and more frustrated.

It was more of the same during the second period. Nine minutes into the period, Nick went into the corner with Balfour in the Lightning's defensive end. He slapped the puck behind the net to Biggie who carried it out of the zone. As Nick followed the play, Balfour speared him in the gut with his stick. Nick swung his stick without thinking, whacking Balfour across the ankles. The referee blew his whistle. "Number seventy-seven. Two minutes for slashing," he said, sending Nick to the penalty box.

The two-minute penalty seemed to last forever but, the Lightning were able to keep the Hollyburn power play at bay. With five minutes left in the second period, the momentum began to shift in the Lightning's favor. They kept the Hawks penned up in their own end, but they couldn't find a way to put the puck in the net. Hollyburn's netminder saved two goals with miraculous stops, and the goalposts saved two more. At the end of two periods, the score was still Hollyburn 1, West Van 0.

Early in the third period, Red redirected Biggie's shot from the point on a power play to tie the game. Three minutes later Cliff Henry banged in a rebound to put the Lightning ahead 2–1. Halfway through the period, Josh Parry tried to free Ivan with a dangerous cross-ice pass. Jamie Balfour intercepted it a few strides inside the Lightning blue line and quickly passed it to his left-winger, who fired it past the Lightning's goalie to even the score.

The goal energized Hollyburn, and the Hawks took control of the game. They kept pressing for the go-ahead goal, but the Lightning's defense was up to the task. With three minutes left in the game, Nick went into the corner in Hollyburn's end with Jamie Balfour. The two fought for control of the puck, but Nick managed to pin it against the boards to force a face-off. When the referee blew his whistle, Balfour shoved his glove in Nick's face. "Call that," Nick yelled at the ref. The ref ignored him.

"You're a wuss, Macklin, just like your old man," Balfour said, elbowing Nick as they skated to the face-off circle.

"Fuck you," Nick said.

"How does it feel, knowing your dad is somebody's bitch?" Balfour sneered.

Nick spun toward Balfour, enraged. He was about to drop his gloves when he realized Balfour was trying to goad him into taking another stupid penalty. He turned away.

"Chickenshit," Balfour said, as Nick took his place at the face-off circle. Balfour lined up opposite him.

Nick concentrated on the referee's hand, blotting everything else out of his mind. As soon as the ref dropped the puck, he stepped across the circle, tied up Balfour's stick with his own, and then kicked the puck back to Josh Parry at the point. It was a trick his dad had taught him. He'd saved it until now.

Parry took two quick steps, then fired a slapshot that grazed the outside of the post. Red raced into the corner and came up with the puck. He slipped it back to Nick who slid it across to Ivan in the slot. Ivan one-timed it past the Hollyburn goalie to give the Lightning the lead.

"Yes," Red roared, as he jumped on Ivan, dragging him to the ice.

Hollyburn refused to give up. They mounted a furious rally, but the Lightning held them off. Final score, West Vancouver 3, Hollyburn 2.

The Lightning were league champions.

The guys stayed at Mike's until closing. They wanted to savor the moment for as long as possible. There was more to it than the fact that they'd won the championship. Nobody said anything, but they all understood that it was the end of a chapter in their lives. They had known each other for more than half their lives and had shared a lot of ups and downs. But that was coming to an end. They were all moving on, heading in different directions.

Ivan's play over the last month had been nothing short of spectacular, convincing the University of Minnesota to give him a full scholarship despite his lack of size. Nick was happy for him, even though he was disappointed that they wouldn't be playing together at UBC. Biggie was going to study business at the University of Victoria. Then he'd take over his dad's clothing store. Google was going to Carleton University in Ottawa to study criminology. Red was the only one who wasn't going to university. He was going to start working at the restaurant.

Nick looked around the table at his friends. They'd keep up with each other, but they wouldn't be together every day like they had been all these years. It wouldn't be the same. Not even close. He was suddenly aware of how much their friendship meant to him. His dad was right. The thing he'd remember most about hockey wouldn't be the championship, it would be the times they'd all spent together. *I'm really going to miss these guys,* he thought. *Even Red.*

CHAPTER FORTY-FIVE

Nick locked his car and joined the crowd streaming toward Rogers Arena for the Canucks game against the Chicago Blackhawks. Coach Phillips had invited him to the game. Nick didn't feel he could turn down the invitation from the UBC coach, but he didn't want to go to the game. He was still angry about the way the Canucks had treated his father. "Don't be silly," his dad had said when he told him. "You're not going to cheer for the owners, are you?"

Nick laughed. "I wasn't planning on it." His dad always said his beef was with management, not the players.

"So go out there and have a good time. That's an order."

"Yes, sir."

His cellphone rang as he turned down West Georgia. It was Sherry. "That was quick," he said. "How was the trip?"

Sherry laughed. Nick had just dropped her and Amy at the airport. They were on their way to Argentina to visit their father for March break. "We're about to board. I just wanted to hear your voice before we left. I'm going to miss you."

"I'm going to miss you too."

"I love you."

"Love you too."

"See you in a week, Macklin. I'll Skype you first chance I get."

"Okay. Have a great time."

"And remember," she said just before they said goodbye to each other, "they're not booing, they're Louing."

Nick laughed. He remembered the first time he took her to a Canucks game. Every time the Canucks goalie, Lou Roberts, made a save, the crowd yelled "Lou. Lou." Sherry thought they were they were saying "Boo. Boo."

"Why are they booing him?" Sherry had asked.

"They're not booing, they're Louing," Nick explained.

"Say what?"

"They're saying Lou, his first name."

"They're not booing, they're Louing," she repeated. "I like that."

Nick smiled at the memory. A feeling of well-being came over him. He remembered something his mother told him once. "Tragedy is part of life. It's going to happen whether you like it or not. The trick in life is to get as much joy as you can." As long as his dad was in jail, tragedy would be part of his life. But as long as he could play hockey, and more importantly, as long as he could be with Sherry, he had plenty to be joyful about too.

"Here you go," Coach Phillips said, passing a bag of popcorn to Nick.

"Thanks, Coach," Nick said. "These are great seats." They were sitting in the tenth row, right at center ice, watching the Canucks and the Blackhawks warm up.

"My pleasure, Nick," Phillips said. "Hope we get a good one."

The referee blew his whistle, summoning the teams to center ice for the opening faceoff. As soon as the puck was dropped, any questions Nick had about who he was going to root for vanished. He'd been a Canucks fan all his life. It was in his blood. Like his dad said, the game was all about the players, not the owners.

It had been a long time since Nick had seen an NHL game in person and it was a completely different experience from watching on TV. You might get a closer look at the action in your living room—although the view from Coach Phillips' seats was pretty damn good—but the game didn't come alive the way it did when you heard the sound of skates carving into the ice, the crunch of bodies slammed against the boards, the shouts of the players calling out to their teammates. You had to be there to appreciate just how talented the players were. With a little imagination it was possible to picture yourself out on the ice when you watched a game on TV, but when you were in the arena, and you saw how fast the players skated and how hard they hit, you understood why, out of the millions who played hockey around the world, only a handful were good enough to wear an NHL uniform.

The game was a tight defensive battle from the start. With two minutes left in regulation time and Vancouver clinging to a 3-2 lead, the Blackhawks mounted a furious charge, pinning the Canucks in their own end. Nick was on his feet along with everyone else in the packed arena, holding his breath every time Chicago fired a shot on goal, and shouting "Lou, Lou," each time Roberts turned them aside.

Twenty-one thousand fans roared with joy when the final buzzer sounded. As Nick and Coach Phillips slowly made their way out of the arena, a short stocky man wearing a leather Canucks jacket came up beside them. "Hey Coach," the man said to Phillips.

"How you doing, Donny?" The two men shook hands.

"I'm good. How good was Roberts tonight?" he said.

"He's the best. Say hello to Nick Macklin. He's coming to play for me next year." He turned to Nick. "This is Donny Jackson. He played goal for us a few years back."

"More than a few," Donny said. He shook hands with Nick. "Macklin," he said to Nick. "Any relation to Steve?"

"He's my dad," Nick said. The familiar awkward silence followed.

"You look like him," Donny said finally.

"He sees the ice the way his dad did, too," Phillips said. "Did you get my email?" he asked.

"I wanted to speak to you about that. You got a minute?"

"Yeah," Phillips said. "I'll see you later, Nick," he said. "I'll be in touch about summer camp." Phillips had offered Nick a coaching job at his summer camp.

"Okay, Coach," Nick said. "And thanks again."

"My pleasure."

"Nice meeting you," Donny said.

"You too," Nick answered.

Nick exited through Gate 10 and joined the lineup at a hot dog stand outside the arena, protected from the rain by an overhang. Off to the side a couple of fans were dressing their hot dogs. The one facing him had the thickest glasses Nick had ever seen. The one with his back to him was wearing a Montreal Canadiens jacket and a red baseball cap. The man took his cap off and scratched his head. He was bald. Nick kept his eyes on him, waiting for him to turn around so he could get a look at his face. It was an automatic response, something he did every time he saw a bald man, and something he'd probably keep on doing as long as his dad was in jail.

"Our guys better start scoring, or we're going to be in

deep shit," the one with the glasses said. "Roberts can't do it all by himself. Did you see the game Thursday?"

"No. I just blew into town today," the bald guy answered. He had a raspy voice that reminded Nick of his grandfather. He coughed—a gut-clearing cough that sounded like it dislodged major organs. He still hadn't turned around.

"Where are you from?" the man with the Coke-bottle glasses asked.

"Down east," the bald man croaked.

"Guess you're used to this kind of weather."

"Everybody says that, but we don't get that much rain in Halifax," he answered. He coughed again, then spat on the sidewalk. *There goes a lung,* Nick thought. "See you later," the bald guy said.

"Take it easy."

Nick watched the man walk away. He didn't get a look at his face, but he didn't need to. The man didn't limp.

"What can I get you?" the hot dog vendor asked, when Nick reached the front of the line.

"Polish sausage," he said, "and a Coke." The vendor took a sausage out of a Tupperware container, made a few cuts in it with a knife and put it on the grill. He handed a can of Coke to Nick who moved aside so the next customer could place his order.

"One Polish sausage," the vendor said a couple of minutes later. Nick helped himself to the condiments, then jogged across the street and walked east on Expo Blvd., heading for his car. Up ahead, the bald man with the raspy voice stood at the corner of Expo and Abbott, hailing a cab. A taxi coming south on Abbott pulled up in front of him. The bald man got into the back seat. As Nick arrived at the corner, the back window of the taxi lowered. The bald man looked out at Nick. Nick froze on the spot—and stared at the round face with no eyebrows. There was no mistaking that face. He'd have known it anywhere. The bald man gave him a friendly nod, and before Nick could react, the taxi took off.

"Stop!" Nick screamed, as he raced after the cab. The taxi was halfway down the block by the time he crossed the street. Nick stared after it uselessly. The same thought kept running through his mind. *He doesn't limp. He doesn't limp.*

CHAPTER FORTY-SIX

Nick crossed the Lion's Gate Bridge and turned onto Taylor Way, on his way back to Al and Helen's place. All this time they'd been on a wild goose chase. *A fake limp*, he thought. *No wonder they hadn't found Baldy.* It was depressing to think that all the time he'd spent looking for him—all those countless hours—had been a complete waste of time.

But by the time he turned into the driveway, his spirits had lifted. Learning that Baldy didn't limp wasn't a setback, he realized. Far from it. It was good news. They had eliminated all the responses to the newspaper advertisement because none of the potential suspects limped. Now that they knew Baldy didn't limp, any one of the suspects they'd written off could be the man they were looking for.

The Lexus was parked in the driveway. Nick jumped out of his car and ran into the house. Al wasn't on the main floor. Nick raced up the stairs. "Al!" he yelled.

"I'm in the washroom," Al shouted back. The phone rang in Al's office. "Get that for me, will you?" Al shouted again. "I'm expecting a call from Stevie." As in Stevie Lyons. Normally Nick would be excited to talk to the best player in the NHL, but this wasn't a normal situation.

Nick went into Al's office and picked up the phone. "Hello."

"Hey Al. It's J.R. I just blew into town today." The

expression was familiar. So was the raspy voice. The caller was seized by a violent coughing spasm. "What's the matter?" J.R. rasped when he stopped coughing. "Cat got your tongue?" Nick stared at the phone in disbelief.

"Who is it?" Al asked as he came into the office. Nick handed him the phone, unable to speak. "Hello?" Al said. A look of surprise flitted across his face. "Hang on," he said. He looked at Nick. "Did you want to tell me something?"

"It was nothing," Nick said. He stood there for a second and then left the room. His brain was racing a mile a minute. *Why is Baldy, if J.R. is Baldy*—and Nick was a hundred per cent positive he was—*calling Al?*

Five minutes later Nick was pacing around his room still asking himself the same question. *Why was Baldy calling Al?* There had to be an innocent explanation. It was insane to think that Al was involved in Albertson's murder. The fact that he knew Baldy had to be a coincidence. *That must be it*, Nick thought. They had always thought that Baldy was involved in hockey in some way. There wasn't much that went on in the hockey world that didn't involve Al. *It's just a coincidence*, he told himself.

Nick started to calm down and felt some of the tension flow out of his body. He remembered how quick he'd been to suspect McAndrew—and how wrong he'd been.

The front door slammed shut. Nick looked out his window and saw Al hurrying down the path. He was about to call out to him when he suddenly remembered that Al had seen Baldy's picture in the newspaper. *If Al knew who he was, why didn't he say something then?* There was only one explanation. And it wasn't an innocent one. Nick watched the Lexus back out of the driveway and speed away.

A fake limp. Nick shook his head. *It was brilliant,* he had to admit it. *Frigging brilliant. Only someone with a devious mind like Al could come up with that.*

He tried to remember what J.R. and the guy with the thick glasses had talked about at the hot dog stand. J.R. wasn't from Vancouver, Nick remembered. "Just blew into town," he said. They talked about the weather, something about Baldy being used to the rain. "Down East," he said. He came from down East, the East Coast. People in BC live out West. People from the Atlantic provinces live down East.

Nick sat down in front of his computer and opened the email account where all the responses to the ad were stored. He was hoping to find an email from the East Coast.

It didn't take him long to find one. I saw the picture in the Halifax Herald. The guy you're looking for is Joe Rossiter. *Joe Rossiter. J.R. Bingo.* As soon as he saw the word *Halifax,* Nick remembered that J.R. said he was from there. He read the rest of the email. He lives in the apartment building on Gerrish Street where my brother Lenny lives. I know you have to check this out but he's is your guy. No doubt about it. If you speak to Lenny, don't tell him about the reward. He'll insist I give him a piece and I don't see why he should get anything.

Nick wondered if they should pay the reward even though he found J.R. on his own, but he didn't spend a lot of time thinking about it. He opened his browser and googled *Hawkins* and *Rossiter,* hoping to find a connection between them. Nothing.

He picked up the phone to call Cuthbert. Then he put it back down. He wasn't sure he could trust him. After all, it was Al who recommended they hire Cuthbert. He was probably being paranoid, he thought, but he decided to wait until he spoke to his dad at the prison the next day before he did anything. He would know what to do.

He undressed and got into bed. He was dead tired, but he was too excited to fall asleep right away. He remembered the other times his hopes had been raised—when he thought McAndrew had killed Albertson, when his dad had identified Baldy's picture—and how disappointed he'd been when nothing came of them. But this was different. He knew who Baldy was, where he lived, and who was behind it all. Once again, the picture of his father walking out of prison passed through his mind's eye.

He was just about to drift off to sleep when he heard Al's car pull into the driveway. A few seconds later, Al was walking up the stairs. Nick looked at the clock on his bedside table. It was 3:30 in the morning. He wondered if Al had been with J.R. all this time. And he wondered what his dad would say when he found out that his oldest friend had framed him for the murder of Marty Albertson.

CHAPTER FORTY-SEVEN

Helen and Al were in the kitchen when Nick came downstairs the next morning. Helen was sipping a cup of tea and watching a morning talk show on TV. Al's head was buried in the newspaper. Nick felt a murderous rage sweep over him. He imagined himself grabbing hold of Al's fat head and smashing it on the counter until it cracked open, the kind of thing they do in the movie with special effects, except he wouldn't need any special effects.

"Good morning," Helen said in a cheery voice.

"Morning," Nick grunted. He looked down and saw that his fists were clenched. He unclenched them as he walked over to the pantry.

Al looked up from his paper. "Hell of a game last night. You picked a good one," he said with a smile.

Nick stared at Al silently.

"Are you okay?" Helen asked.

"I'm fine," Nick snapped.

Al gave Nick a curious look. "Somebody woke up on the wrong side of the bed," he said. Nick poured himself a bowl of granola.

Helen stood up. "I've got to go or I'll be late for my yoga class. Say hello to your dad for me. She bent down and kissed Al on the top of his head. "Bye, sweetie."

"Bye-bye."

Nick sat at the table with his bowl of cereal and

focused on the TV. Al put down the newspaper and got up. "We'll leave in ten minutes," he said.

"Okay," Nick said, trying to keep his voice neutral. He was aware that Al was looking at him, but he didn't trust himself to look up. He was afraid he might give himself away, so he kept his eyes on the TV until Al left the kitchen. He wished Helen was taking him to the prison. Two hours there and two hours back, alone in a car with the man who put his father in jail. Nick didn't know if he could handle it.

As Nick got up to put his bowl in the dishwasher, the morning news came on the TV. "Early this morning a man's body was found floating in False Creek. He was identified as Joe Rossiter from Halifax, Nova Scotia. It is the city's twelfth homicide of the year. Police are investigating." At the mention of Rossiter's name, Nick wheeled around to look at the TV. A photo of the bald man with no eyebrows stared back at him.

A car horn blared. "Look out!" Al yelled. Nick jerked the steering wheel and veered back into the right lane. The driver to his left honked his horn once more, and then sped off. "Pay attention to what you're doing," Al barked.

They were approaching the exit to Agassiz. Nick didn't remember a thing about the drive. He'd spent the entire trip going over the facts again and again, trying to see if he'd missed anything. But they always led to the same conclusion. Al Hawkins had killed Marty Albertson, and framed his father for the murder.

The facts were straightforward. A couple of hours before Nick and Google saw the man they now knew was Baldy at the Giants game, Nick overheard Al on the phone, royally pissed, agreeing to meet someone at eight-thirty.

Then Nick had seen Al hand a bald man a wad of cash. He remembered that he'd momentarily thought the man was Baldy, until he saw that he didn't limp. So he assumed that Al had started gambling again. Fast-forward to yesterday, when Nick saw Baldy at the Canucks game and found out that the limp was a trick. An hour later J.R. aka Baldy calls Al. A few hours after that, he's found floating in False Creek.

It all added up. Al paid J.R. to put the paint on his dad's jacket, but J.R. must have kept demanding more money. Al paid him off once—at the Giants game—but when J.R. contacted him again he realized the demands were never going to stop. So he killed him. It was the only explanation that fit the facts. The problem was that Nick couldn't prove it. And now, the one person who could had just disappeared. Permanently.

He glanced over at Al. "Who cares if he can't skate? You're paying him for his fists, not his feet. He loves it in Colorado. But half the GMs in the league are interested in him, so if you want to keep him, you're going to have to loosen the purse strings." *Business as usual,* Nick thought. It was incredible. Less than twelve hours ago Al had murdered a man in cold blood and here he was, wheeling and dealing as if nothing had happened.

Nick pulled into the prison parking lot. He was so anxious to see his father, it almost hurt.

A small crowd of visitors stood by the front door. Nick checked the car clock. It was 8:50. Visiting hours started in ten minutes. He wondered why everyone was still outside. He and Al got out of the car and walked toward the entrance.

"What's going on?" Al asked a large woman standing off to the side with a little boy.

"Lockdown," she said. "There was a riot last night. An inmate was killed."

"Did they say who it was?" Nick asked anxiously.

"His name was Michael Edwards."

Nick breathed a sigh of relief. "When are they going to let us in?"

The fat lady shook her head. "They're not. They told us to go home."

"But I have to see my dad," he said. The lady shrugged.

"We might as well get going," Al said. "No point sticking around."

"Not until I found out what's going on," Nick said angrily. Al held his hands up in mock surrender.

Nick saw Pete standing by the front entrance. He walked over to him. "Is my dad all right?" he asked.

"He's fine, Nick."

"What happened? The lady over there said someone got killed during a riot last night."

Pete nodded. "A group of inmates started a fight in the gym and one of them was stabbed to death. Two officers were injured trying to restore order. They're both in the hospital."

"Was my dad there?"

"No."

"Can I see him? It's really important."

"Not a chance, Nick. All inmates are confined to their cells until further notice."

"When will I be able to see him?"

"Hard to say. I've been here eleven years and this was the worst disturbance I've ever seen. It could be a couple of weeks. Maybe more."

"Can he phone me?"

"Not until the lockdown's lifted."

"When will that be?"

"I told you, I don't know. It's not going to happen anytime soon, that's for sure. Two of our own got hurt. One's in pretty bad shape. Nobody's going to be in a hurry to do any favors for the inmates. Best thing is to give us a call in a few days. Hopefully we'll know more then. Okay?"

Pete walked away. "Let's go, Nick," Al said, putting his hand on his shoulder. Nick shrugged it off and started walking toward the car. If he was going to prove that Al Hawkins killed Marty Albertson, he'd have to do it on his own.

CHAPTER FORTY-EIGHT

Nick watched from his bedroom window until Al's car disappeared from sight. He and Helen had gone shopping. They'd be away from the house for at least an hour. He turned to Google. "Let's go," he said.

They hurried into Al's office. His computer was shut down. Google hit the power button on the computer tower. Nick opened Al's filing cabinet as they waited for the computer to boot up. The cabinet squeaked loudly. *Needs oil*, he thought. He leafed through all of Al's files. There was one for each client. Nick found the one labeled Marty Albertson and took it out of the drawer.

"Shit," Google said. Nick looked at the screen. A dialogue box asked for a password. "Do you know his password?" Google asked.

Nick shook his head. "Now what?"

"No problem," Google said. "We can buy a hidden camera and record him when he logs on."

"You've been watching too many Bond movies. Where are we going to get a hidden camera?" Nick asked.

"The Spyzone on West Pender," Google said, as he shut down Al's computer. Nick rifled through Albertson's file. There wasn't anything of interest in it. Just his last contract with the Leafs and some financial statements.

He replaced the file. The cabinet squeaked again. Then the two of them went back to Nick's bedroom.

Google sat down at Nick's laptop, opened his browser, and found the store's website. "Look," he said. "They've got all kinds of cameras." Nick looked over Google's shoulder at the screen. They had cameras hidden in just about anything you could think of: clocks, sunglasses, plants, purses, smoke alarms, even a teddy bear.

"This is the one we want," Google said, pointing to a picture of a book camera. "We can put it on the bookshelf beside Al's desk. The camera's hidden in the spine of the book. There's a tiny hole in the cover. You wouldn't notice it unless you were looking for it."

An hour later Nick and Google walked into Spyzone. An elderly woman was standing behind the counter.

"Can I help you?" she asked.

"We'd like to buy a hidden book camera," Nick said.

"We want one that's wireless, with a built-in recorder," Google added.

"Color or black and white?" she asked.

"Black and white is fine," Nick said.

"I'll see if we have one in stock." She went over to her computer. "You're in luck," she said a few seconds later. "We have one left. I'll get it for you."

"Thanks," Nick said. The women went through a door at the back of the store. A few minutes later she returned with a box. She opened it and took out the *International Student Dictionary*. She pointed to a small hole in the spine. "That's where the lens is," she said. Nick peered at it. Google was right. You'd never know it was there.

"How do you turn it on?" Nick asked.

"Right here," she said, pointing to a small switch. The video is recorded on a hidden memory card." She opened the book. The memory card was in an opening carved into the pages. "The memory card comes with an adaptor with a USB port so you can plug it into your computer."

"Cool," Google said. "How long does it record for?"

"Up to twenty hours."

"This is perfect," Google said.

"How much does it cost?" Nick asked.

"Seven ninety-nine plus tax," she said. "It's our top-of-the-line model. I can order one that's less expensive if you don't need all the bells and whistles, but it will take a week or so to come in."

"We need it now," Nick said. He opened his wallet and handed the woman his credit card. *We better find something on Al's computer,* he thought, *or Dad will hit the roof when he sees the next credit card statement.*

It was five-thirty by the time Nick got back to the house. There was a note from Helen in the kitchen. "We've gone to Jesse's for dinner. There's some roast chicken and a green bean and almond salad in the fridge."

Nick went up to Al's office. He opened the dictionary, turned on the camera and put the dictionary on the bookshelf beside Al's desk. Then he sat down at Al's computer and pretended he was typing in a password. When he was done he took the memory card out of the book, went into his room, put the card in the adaptor and plugged it into his laptop.

The video loaded automatically. The camera angle was perfect, but Nick couldn't tell which keys his fingers were hitting. He went back to the start of the recording and hit the pause button each time his finger hit a key. When he zoomed in, he could see which letter he was touching. *This will work,* he thought.

He returned to Al's office and put the memory card

back in the book. Then he went downstairs to the kitchen and polished off the roast chicken.

He had started in on the salad when he heard Al and Helen come through the front door. He hoped they'd go straight upstairs, but they must have seen the light on in the kitchen. He felt himself tense as he heard their footsteps approaching. "Oh, good," Helen said, "you found my note. How was the chicken?"

"Great," Nick said, looking up from the salad for a brief second. He couldn't bear to look at Al any longer than that.

"You have to ask?" Al said, gesturing at the plate where a few bones were all that was left of the chicken. "It looks like a pack of vultures got at it." Nick eyed his dinner knife and imagined sticking it into Al's fat face.

"Did you call the prison today?" Al asked.

"Yeah." Or better yet, he'd stick it into his eyeball.

"Well," Al said impatiently, "are they still in lockdown?"

"Yeah." And cram it down his throat.

"When's it going to end?"

"Don't know."

"I'll make a couple of calls tomorrow," Al said. "See what I can find out."

Nick didn't bother to answer. Out of the corner of his eye he saw Al give Helen a questioning look, as if to say "What's wrong with him?"

"Good night, honey," Helen said. "See you in the morning."

"Night," Nick grunted without looking up.

Al and Helen left the kitchen. "Teenagers," he heard Al say. "The best thing you can say about them is that they grow out of it."

CHAPTER FORTY-NINE

Nick's alarm clock went off at five a.m. He turned it off, scrambled out of bed and hurried into the hallway. The door to Al and Helen's bedroom was closed. He put his ear to it, making sure they were still asleep. Silence. He crept into Al's office, opened the dictionary, and turned on the camera.

The floor creaked behind him. His stomach leaped into his throat. He wheeled around, but it was only Alfie. The cat stared at him, then padded out of the room. Nick quickly put the dictionary back into position on the bookshelf, then crept back to his bedroom. He closed the door behind him. He felt like a character in a movie. Except if this *was* a movie, Al would have caught him red-handed. "Looking for something to read?" he would have said as the camera zoomed in on his evil smile.

Of course in the movies Nick would have come up with a good reason why he was in Al's office, or if he couldn't come up with a good reason, he'd come up with a bad one that Al would be stupid enough to buy. It didn't work like that in real life. In real life Nick wouldn't have come up with a good reason for him to be in Al's office because there wasn't one. In real life he would have stared stupidly at Al, and then he would have shit his pants. And then ... Nick didn't want to think about what would happen then.

He tried to go back to sleep, but he was too nervous worrying about everything that could go wrong. Al might not go on the computer today. Or he might move the keyboard out of camera range before he logged on. Or, worst of all, he might find the book camera. If that happened, all hell would break loose.

Nick spent the next two hours staring at the ceiling, imagining various nightmare scenarios over and over again, before he finally fell asleep.

Nick woke up a little after nine and got dressed. He walked past Al's office. Al was at his desk. "Got a minute?" he asked, motioning for Nick to come in. Al had a serious expression on his face. Nick could feel the hairs on the back of his neck stand up. The nightmare had come true. Al had found the camera. He went into the office, his legs feeling like rubber. He wracked his brain for a plausible explanation but he couldn't come up with one. All he could do was to deny any knowledge about the camera, and that was not going to wash.

"Are you okay?" Al asked.

"Bad night," Nick said, his voice cracking.

Al gave him a quizzical look. "I called a friend who works in Corrections," he said. "He told me they're not going to lift the lockdown until they finish their investigation."

Nick felt the tension flow out of his body. "How long is that going to take?" he asked. Al's computer was on. He snuck a glance at the dictionary. It was in the bookshelf, right where he'd left it.

The phone rang before Al answered Nick's question. "Hello … Let me look. What year do you want? … Okay. Hang on." Al put the phone down and got to his feet. He walked around the desk to the bookcase. He seemed to be staring right at the dictionary. The words on the binding—*International Student Dictionary*—jumped out at Nick. *Shit,* Nick thought as he realized that Al didn't own a copy of the dictionary. Al reached his hand toward the dictionary. *I'm screwed,* Nick thought. Al's hand continued past the dictionary to the shelf above it. He grabbed a binder and walked back to his desk. He picked up the receiver. "I got it. I'll bring it with me ... Okay, bye." He hung up, then shut down his computer and got to his feet. "What were we talking about?" he asked.

"I can't remember," Nick said. His mind was a blank.

"Oh, yeah. The lockdown," Al said, looking at Nick curiously. "My friend said it's going to last at least another week. He'll see if he can get them to let Steve call you—as a favor to me."

As a favor to me, Nick repeated to himself. He could feel his anger rising. He forced himself to keep his cool. Al looked at his watch. "Gotta get going," he said. He grabbed the binder off his desk.

"See you later," Al said, as they left the room. Nick waited until he heard the front door close, then he returned to Al's office, grabbed the dictionary off the bookshelf, and hurried back into his bedroom.

Nick closed the door, took the memory card out of the book, and placed it in his computer. He pressed fast-forward through the recording, until he saw Al sit down at his desk. Then he pushed the play button. He watched as Al turned on his computer and waited for it to boot up. Less than a minute later Nick had Al's password: DO-RE-MI. He picked up his phone and called Google.

CHAPTER FIFTY

"Come in," Nick said, answering the knock at his bedroom door. He and Google looked up as Helen stepped inside.

"I just came in to say goodbye. Al's taking me to the airport now," Helen said. She was going to a yoga retreat in Hawaii. "There's plenty of food in the fridge, so help yourselves."

"Okay," Nick said.

"Thanks, Mrs. Hawkins," said Google.

"How's the project going?" Helen asked.

"We're nearly done," Nick said.

"Okay. Bye-bye," Helen said. "See you in a week."

"Have fun," Nick said. Helen smiled and closed the door behind her.

"Do you think she knows anything about this?" Google asked.

Nick shook his head. "No way," he said. He remembered how upset Helen was when Al missed his GA meeting. She had no idea he was meeting Baldy.

Nick and Google watched Al's car pull out of the driveway and onto the road. They waited a minute to make sure he wasn't coming back. "Let's go," Nick said. "Did you bring the email retrieval program?"

Google nodded and pointed at his knapsack. They went into Al's office. Google sat down at the desk, turned on the computer and typed in Al's password. "We're in," he said a moment later.

Google searched the hard drive. Marty Albertson's name showed up on dozens of emails.

"We don't have time to go through all of these now," Nick said.

"No problem. I'll forward them to you," Google said. He saved the messages to Hawkins' desktop and sent them to Nick. Then he dragged the emails into the recycle bin and emptied it. "Let's see if he deleted anything." He put the email retrieval disk into the slot on the side of Al's computer.

Albertson's name appeared in three messages that Al had deleted. All three emails were dated September 15, two days before Albertson's murder.

The first was from Albertson to Hawkins.

Went to Manuk Manka. Flew over the entire island in a helicopter. Nothing there, just forest. No sign of any construction. Something's not right.

The second email was Hawkins' response to Albertson, a couple of hours later.

This is very disturbing. Let's talk when you're back in Vancouver. Meanwhile, I'll look into it.

Albertson replied two minutes later.

I'll call you when I get back.

"Does this mean anything to you?" Google asked.

Nick shook his head. "What's Manuk Manka?" he asked.

Google opened the browser and checked it out on Wikipedia. "It's an island in the Philippines."

The Philippines. Nick remembered that Albertson had gone to the Philippines after he was caught playing around with the married woman in Hong Kong. He went into his bedroom, grabbed the detective's report, and hurried back into Al's office.

He flipped through to the page he was looking for. "Albertson was in the Philippines on September 15th," he said to Google, "but there's nothing in here about Manuk Manka. See if it's mentioned anywhere else."

Google ran a search on the computer. In addition to the mention in the deleted emails, Manuk Manka came up in three of the emails that Google had already forwarded to Nick. "Is there anything else we should look for?" he asked.

"Yeah," Nick said. "Joe Rossiter."

Google put the computer through its paces. It took a couple of minutes. Nothing about Rossiter. "Anything else?" he asked.

Nick shook his head. "Let's get out of here." Google nodded. Neither of them wanted to spend a minute more in Al's office than they had to. They both knew what had happened to Marty Albertson and Joe Rossiter.

Back in Nick's bedroom, they opened the three emails that mentioned Manuk Manka. The first was from Al, and as soon as Nick read it, he understood why Albertson had visited the island.

Gentlemen: Construction of the resort on Manuk Manka will begin next month. Once the shovels are in the ground, we'll each owe a final payment of 500 thousand dollars for a total investment of one million dollars each. The bean counters say we'll get our money back in the first year. From then on everything we make will be pure profit. I will keep you posted. Al.

"Look," Google said. "This email was sent to your dad too. And Jameson. And Bryant …

"I know what this is about," Nick said, interrupting him. "Al got Dad and Albertson and a bunch of other clients to invest in a resort in the Philippines. They lost all their money." *A million dollars!* He had no idea his father had lost so much money.

A description and a computer-generated picture of what the resort would look like was attached to the email. Nick had never seen anything like it. Private villas, each with a huge kidney-shaped swimming pool; seven first-class restaurants with spectacular views of the ocean; a state-of-the art exercise complex; and an eighteen-hole championship golf course.

Google opened the next email, also from Hawkins to Nick's dad and the others. As you can see from the pictures, they've started construction on the clubhouse for the golf course. The final payment is now due. Al.

Two photos were attached to the email. The first was of Al, wearing a hard hat and standing in front of a yellow bulldozer in the middle of a huge hole that had been dug for the foundation of the clubhouse. The second was a long shot of Al standing on the edge of the pit beside a couple of palm trees, with the ocean shimmering in the background.

Google opened the third email: another one from Hawkins to the same group. Gentlemen: I'm afraid I have some terrible news. I couldn't get in touch with the contractor so I asked our lawyer in the Philippines to check into it for me. I just heard back from him. The contractor has disappeared. He vanished the day after we made the final payment. There's no trace of him, or our money. We've been swindled. Al.

"You mean everybody lost a million dollars?" Google asked.

"Looks like it."

"What does this have to do with Albertson's murder?" Google asked.

"That's the million dollar question," Nick said. "No pun intended."

Google opened the email Albertson sent Hawkins after he visited the island of Manuk Manka, and read it aloud.

Went to Manuk Manka. Flew over the entire island in a helicopter. There's nothing there, just forest. No sign of any construction. Something's not right.

"No sign of any construction," Google repeated. He opened up on one of the pictures, the long shot of Al standing at the edge of the hole for the foundation of the clubhouse. The hole was enormous. "How could you go over a tiny island in a helicopter and miss seeing that?" Google asked.

"You couldn't," Nick said. "Let's see the other picture." Google clicked on it. There was Al, in the bottom of the hole, standing beside a bulldozer. "This doesn't make any sense," Nick said. The two of them stared at the picture. "I don't get it," he said.

"I think I do," Google said. He hit Control +, zooming in on the bulldozer. He hit the keys again ... and again. "Look at that," he said.

"Look at what?"

"The license plate."

It was a little out of focus but Nick could still read it. BEAUTIFUL BRITISH COLUMBIA. He looked up at Google. "What the ... "

"Photoshop," Google said. "The picture was taken in BC. There was no resort. It was a scam. Al ripped everybody off. Albertson found out about it ..."

"… and that's why Al killed him."

Nick and Google stared at each other. "I still don't understand one thing," Nick said after a few moments. "Albertson knew my father lost money on the resort." Google nodded. "But when he called him after he came back from the Philippines, he said he wanted to talk about the hit. He didn't say a word about the resort. It doesn't make sense."

"You're right," Google agreed. "We have to go to the cops with this, Nick."

"We can't."

"Why not? This proves Al stole the money."

"That's all it proves. It doesn't prove he killed Albertson. And if we can't prove that, we won't get Dad out of jail."

CHAPTER FIFTY-ONE

Nick woke up at six-thirty. He got out of bed and went into Al's office. He didn't know if the plan would work, but he and Google had looked at it from every angle, and they hadn't come up with anything better.

He opened the top drawer of Al's filing cabinet. It squeaked loudly. He waited a few seconds, then closed the drawer. It squeaked again. He opened it again, waited, and closed it. *Squeak ... Squeak.* A few seconds later, he heard Al's bedroom door open and close. Footsteps came toward the office. Nick was walking toward the door when Al came in.

"What are you doing in here?" he asked.

"Uh ... uh." Nick mumbled. "... I was looking for some staples. I'm out."

"Did you find them?"

"No."

"They're right here," Al said, pointing to his desk. A box of staples was in plain view. He picked them up. "They may not be the right size," he said, looking at the box.

"I'll check," Nick said, putting out his hand.

"That's okay," Al said. He walked out of the office and into Nick's bedroom. Nick followed. His stapler was on his desk. And so was a box of staples. Al pointed at it and gave Nick a questioning look.

"Don't know how I missed that," Nick said.

"These things happen," Al said. "Good night."

"Good night."

As soon as Al left his bedroom, Nick was on the phone with Google. "I don't know if he suspects anything," he said after telling Google what happened. "It's hard to tell. I guess I'll find out tonight."

"You sure you want to go through with this?" Google asked.

"I have to, Goog. It's the only way we're ever going to prove that he killed Albertson."

"I know. But I don't have to like it."

Sherry Skyped Nick a few minutes after Google signed off. "Hey stranger. What's new?" she said, when her smiling face appeared on the screen.

The smile disappeared in a hurry. "Oh my God," she said after Nick filled her in on what had happened in the four days since she left for Argentina. There was a long pause. "Oh my God," she repeated. Another pause. "What are you going to do?"

Nick told her. Sherry didn't like his plan any better than Google did. But she admitted there was nothing else he could do.

"Be careful," she warned.

"I will," he promised.

"Call me as soon as you know anything," she said. He nodded. "I love you, Nick," she said softly.

"I love you too." Nick knew Sherry was thinking the same thing he was. If his plan didn't work, they might never see each other again.

CHAPTER FIFTY-TWO

Nick's alarm went off at 3 a.m., waking him out of a deep sleep. He'd been dreaming about something pleasant, but the details vanished the moment he awoke. He got out of bed and put on his jeans and a sweatshirt. He grabbed the tape recorder he and Google bought at SpyZone earlier in the day, set it to the voice activation mode and put it in the pocket of his sweatshirt. Then he opened the door to his bedroom and snuck into Al's office.

He turned on Al's computer and keyed in his password. Then he went over to the filing cabinet and opened and closed it. It seemed to squeak louder than it had before. He went back to the computer and ran a search for *Rossiter.*

"Find anything interesting?"

Nick whirled around in his seat. Al was standing in the doorway. He walked over to the computer and looked at the dialogue box on the screen. SEARCHING FOR FILES CONTAINING THE WORD ROSSITER, he read. He looked at Nick. "You won't find anything about Joe Rossiter here," he said, shaking his head sadly.

Didn't expect to, Nick thought. "I know you killed him," he said. "And Albertson too."

Al didn't bother to deny it. "How the hell did you figure that out?" he asked.

Nick wondered if that would be considered a confession in a court of law. He silently prayed that the tape recorder was working. He knew Al was guilty, but he didn't have any proof. He needed Al to confess if he was going to get his dad out of jail. "I saw Rossiter at a Canucks game the night you killed him. I recognized him from his photo, and then I recognized his voice when he called you."

"I should have guessed something was up," Al said. "You've been acting pretty weird lately." He gazed at Nick. Nick stared back with undisguised hatred in his eyes. "You think this makes a difference? You can't prove anything," Al said. "Nobody's going to believe you."

Maybe not, Nick said to himself, *but they'll believe you.* "Rossiter was blackmailing you, wasn't he? That's why you killed him."

"Joe had been well paid. He made the mistake of getting greedy." *That's more like it,* Nick thought. "What else do you know?" Al asked.

"I know you killed Albertson because he found out about the resort scam when he went to the Philippines."

"I'm impressed," Al said.

"Did you really need the money that badly?"

"You don't understand. I didn't want to do it. I didn't have a choice. My life was at stake. So was Helen's."

"Bullshit," Nick said.

"I owed some people a lot of money—gambling debts. They said if I didn't pay up, they'd kill both of us. Everything was fine until Marty got nosy. Helen and I had our lives back. Steve and the others lost some money, but it wasn't anything they couldn't afford. Then Marty went and ruined it all. I didn't want to have to involve your father in this. I really didn't."

"Don't you dare say that!" Nick shouted.

"I had to do it," Al said calmly. "Otherwise the police

would have kept looking for a suspect. I couldn't take that chance. Somebody had to take the rap. Your dad was the logical choice. He had the motive. I just had to make it look like he had the opportunity."

"What are you talking about?"

"The police had to believe your father had a meeting with Marty, or I wouldn't have been able to pin the murder on him."

"What do you mean? Albertson called Dad to arrange the meeting."

"Albertson never called your father."

"You're out of your fucking mind."

"You're out of your fucking mind," Al repeated, imitating Nick's voice perfectly. "You're a smart boy. Figure it out."

"Oh my God," Nick said. *That explains why Albertson didn't tell Dad about the real estate scam. He wasn't the one who phoned him.* "You called Dad and pretended to be Albertson." Nick felt like his head was going to explode

Al held his hand up to his face, thumb and pinky extended, as if he were on the phone. "Hello, Steve," he said, mimicking Albertson's deep voice. "It's Marty Albertson here. It's time we talked about what happened … To be honest, I wasn't sure Steve would agree to meet with Marty," Al said in his normal voice.

He made the pretend phone gesture again. "Let me get a pen and paper to write down the directions to your house," he said, once again sounding like Albertson. Al reverted to his normal voice. "Of course I changed the location of the meeting when I put it in Marty's BlackBerry. "So when your dad told the police he and Marty were supposed to meet at his house in West Van, they were convinced he was lying. And the rest, as they say, is history."

Nick glared at him. But inwardly he was jubilant. *Thanks for tying up all the loose ends, asshole,* he said to himself.

"I have two questions for you," Al said. "First of all, did you really think I was going to fall for that clumsy act with the stapler?"

"What do you mean?"

"It took all of three seconds to figure out why a smart kid like you would make up such a dumb story. You wanted me to be suspicious of you. You didn't come in here tonight hoping to find anything. You wanted me to catch you in here, you wanted me to hear you open that squeaky filing cabinet." Nick didn't say anything. "You knew I was involved in Albertson's murder, but you didn't have any proof. You needed a confession." Al yawned. "Sorry. I don't do as well without a good night's sleep as I used to," he said.

He reached into his jacket pocket and took out a gun. "Turn around and put your hands behind your back," he ordered. Nick did as he was told. Al pulled a pair of handcuffs from a second pocket and snapped them on Nick's wrists. He put his hand on Nick's shoulder, spun him around, and patted him down with his free hand. It didn't take long to find the tape recorder. Al shook his head as if he was disappointed in Nick for being so stupid. He dropped the recorder in his jacket pocket, and steered Nick toward the door.

"You said you had two questions," Nick said.

"Thanks for reminding me," Al replied. "Exactly what did you think was going to happen after you got your confession? Did you think I was just going to let you go?"

CHAPTER FIFTY-THREE

Al marched Nick into the kitchen. "You should have minded your own business, Nick."

"Fuck you."

Al took a bottle of Scotch out of the cupboard. "All that money spent on public service announcements, and you still can't stop kids from drinking and driving." He opened the utility drawer and took out a roll of duct tape. "Helen is going to be devastated when she hears about the accident. She really cares about you." He ripped off a strip of the tape and stuck it over Nick's mouth. Then he grabbed the bottle of Scotch and put it in a cloth shopping bag. He slung the bag over his shoulder and steered Nick out of the kitchen toward the front door. When they were outside he locked the door, keeping a firm grip on Nick's arm. Then he led him down the front path toward the driveway.

"Rossiter was blackmailing you, wasn't he? That's why you killed him." Nick's voice came from the flower garden on the left side of the path.

"What the … ?" Hawkins said, whirling in the direction of the voice.

"Joe had been well paid. He made the mistake of getting greedy." This time it was Al's voice, and it came from the right side of the path. Al spun in the other direction. *"I didn't want to have to involve your father in this. I really didn't."* Al whirled back

244

to the left. *"Somebody had to take the rap. Your dad was the logical choice."* Google was standing at the foot of the pathway, holding a tape recorder in his hand. *"And the rest, as they say, is history.*

Al reached into his jacket for his gun, but before he could get to it, a massive pair of arms wrapped him in a bear hug from behind.

"You're not going anywhere, pal," said Biggie. Al struggled to free himself, but he might as well have been locked inside a suit of armor. Ivan emerged from the shadows on the left. Red came from the right. They both were holding tape recorders. Ivan took the duct tape off Nick's mouth.

"The key to the handcuffs is in his jacket pocket," Nick said. Ivan reached into Al's pocket. A few seconds later the cuffs were off Nick and on Al.

Nick rubbed his wrists. He looked at Al, at the man who had caused him so much pain, the man who had deprived him of his father, and his father of his freedom, the man who had killed twice in order to save his own skin, the man who would have killed him too, if he could have gotten away with it. Every bone in his body cried out for revenge.

"It's over, Nick," Ivan said softly, as if he had read his mind.

"I know," Nick said. He looked at Al again. Al stared back through dead, defeated eyes. Ivan was right. It was over. Nick turned and took a step down the path. Then he turned back, clenched his fist, drew back his arm, and smashed Al in the face as hard as he could.

CHAPTER FIFTY-FOUR

For the fourth time that morning, the front door of the prison swung open. For the fourth time, someone other than Nick's dad walked through it. Nick could have waited inside the prison, but he was never going in there again. He'd had more than enough of that place for a lifetime. He took a deep breath, trying to calm himself.

The sun peeked through the clouds. It had been raining since he left Vancouver, but now it looked like the day would be nice. *It isn't just going to be a nice day,* Nick thought. *It's going to be a great day. The greatest ever.*

His nightmare was coming to an end.

The authorities had taken less than a month from the time Al was arrested to arrange his dad's release. It normally took much longer to get a wrongly convicted person out of jail, but once the story broke, the public demanded that Nick's dad be freed. The politicians responded to the pressure by fast-tracking the case through the system.

Nick became an instant celebrity. He was besieged with interview requests from news media and talk shows in Canada and the United States. CNN ran a half-hour special on the story. The first few times he was on TV were exciting, but it didn't take long before he grew tired of everybody wanting a piece of him. After a while he stopped returning the phone calls. He just wanted things to get back to normal.

His dad had been furious when he found out that Al was behind everything. It was a good thing Al was being held in a different prison—a maximum-security institution in Edmonton—or Nick's dad might actually have committed a murder. But all those hours of meditation kicked in, and eventually Nick's father calmed down. "I'm not going to waste energy dwelling on the past," he said to Nick the last time he visited him. "Al got what he deserved"—life in prison without parole—"so let's just leave it at that." That was his way of telling Nick he didn't want to talk about Al any more. Nick went along with his dad's wishes, but that didn't stop him from shaking with rage whenever he thought about what Al had done to them.

It had been a long wait but the story had a happy ending for Nick and his dad. That wasn't the case for Helen. She called Nick a week or so after Al was arrested. She told him she had filed for a divorce and was moving away from Vancouver. Nick wasn't surprised she was going away. It would be impossible for her to keep living here, where everybody knew who she was.

Helen told Nick she wanted to see him before she left. The two met at a café near his school. Nick almost didn't recognize her when she walked in; she'd aged twenty years. She told him that she was sorry for the pain Al had caused Nick and his dad. "We were married for thirty-nine years," she said. "And I had no idea who he really was. I feel like such a fool." A tear trickled down her cheek. Then she stood up, told Nick she hoped he'd have a wonderful life, gave him a hug, and left the café.

A week later, Helen drove to the prison to say goodbye to Nick's dad in person. She told him that she'd visited Al before he was taken to Edmonton to tell him to his face that neither she nor any of the kids would ever see him or speak to him again. "Serves him right," Nick said, when his father told him. "Yes it does," his dad answered.

The front door of the prison opened again. Another false alarm.

His dad had called the day before to tell him he was being released. There had been no advance warning. As soon as Nick got off the phone he ran downstairs to tell Sherry the good news. He had moved in with her and her family after Al was arrested. Nick and Sherry had stayed up all night talking, but Nick couldn't remember what they'd talked about. Everything that happened after the phone call from his dad was a blur. Early in the morning Nick threw his clothes into his suitcase. He left for the prison around eight. Sherry walked him to the car. He put his suitcase in the trunk. The two looked at each other without speaking for a moment. They had spent so much time together in the past month that it felt weird to know that he wouldn't be coming back to the house that night. "I'll call you," he said finally. "Say hi to your dad," Sherry said. Nick nodded. Then he got into the car and drove away. Through the rear-view mirror he could see her standing on the sidewalk.

The front door to the prison opened yet again. This time Nick's father came through it, pulling a suitcase behind him. The scene Nick had imagined so many times since his dad had gone to prison was finally happening—for real. His father stopped just outside the door. He saw Nick and held his arms out. Nick raced toward him. The two embraced wordlessly, holding on to each other for a long time before they separated.

"Let's go home, son," his dad said. Nick nodded. It didn't matter that they were going to a hotel. Nick knew what his father meant. They walked to the parking lot. Nick pushed a button on his key, unlocking the car doors. When his dad reached the passenger side, he looked back at the prison for a few seconds, as if he wanted to engrave the image on his memory. Then he opened the door and got into the car.

They talked non-stop all the way to Vancouver, but only about the future. By the time they entered the city, the prison seemed like a distant memory. Nick pulled into the right lane as soon as he saw the sign for the West 2nd Avenue exit that led to their hotel on Granville Island. They would stay there until they found a place to live.

"Keep going," his dad said. Fifteen minutes later they were standing in front of a tombstone at the Capilano View Cemetery.

Nick stared at the inscription. ELIZABETH MACKLIN, BELOVED MOTHER AND WIFE.

His dad placed a yellow rose in front of the tombstone. "Yellow was her favorite color, remember?"

"I do," Nick said.

ACKNOWLEDGEMENTS

I would like to express my appreciation to the many people who helped me during the writing of this book.

First, thank you to my family and friends who read the manuscript. Their responses were gratifying, and their feedback invaluable: my daughter Laura, my parents, Irving and Lita-Rose, and my brother Gordon, as well as Nicolas, Zacharie, Steven, Shannon, Monique, Ivan, Gary, Charlie, Joanne, and Dan.

Thanks also, to my friend Jake Onrot for his enthusiasm and steadfast encouragement. And a special thank you to my friend and fellow writer, Peter Busby, for an insightful analysis of the manuscript and for his moral support throughout.

I am grateful to Hans Angel for providing information about Kent Institution in Agassiz, BC, and to Sandra Leonard and John Conroy for sharing their knowledge of the Canadian penal system.

Special thanks go to my wonderful editor, Lynne Missen, and the rest of the team at Penguin Canada. My agent Patricia Ocampo at TLA deserves a huge thank you for her patience, good advice, and for her faith in me and in my story.

And finally, I would like to thank my wife, Claudette Jaiko. I would not have been able to write this book without her unwavering encouragement and support.

I would be delighted to hear from readers. Please feel free to contact me by email: mbetcherman@gmail.com

ſ

48445219R00144

Made in the USA
Lexington, KY
31 December 2015